SILVER EYED SEER

LEGENDARY STARS SAGA BOOK TWO

DAI'JA S. ROSE

NOVA INK BOOKS

SILVER EYED SEER

Legendary Stars Saga Book Two

Dai'Ja S. Rose

Nova Ink Books

To all of you feverishly chasing your destiny.

Kashmala

Wyndhm

Snow Tribe

Beach Tribe

HEYRA

Lower Ember

Jungle Tribe

Upper Ember

Kindle

PYROC

Mystic Ocean

BOOKTOK PRAISE

"This book was a breath of fresh air for fantasy readers. I'm excited to read more of the Legends story!" – @mblazer21

"Prepare to be captivated by this debut fantasy novel brimming with enchanting magic and extraordinary characters. Eagerly awaiting the sequel." – @bookswithambs

"Jai's character had me hooked from the very beginning! Navigating his impossible fate and accepting the reality of his new found purpose was an exhilarating journey. This is one for those who struggle to find intention and those ever faced with a life or death choice. " – @bookbehavior

"The Golden Eyed Legend is a riveting new fantasy series that I simply could not put down!" – @laurenslibraryyy

"Fun, adventurous, and fiery. It was a fast-paced, action pack. Our story is set in a world where some have lost their magic and others have kept and nurtured it. The story centers on a young man named Jai who was orphaned and taken in at a young age. One day he finds out he was gifted with a great power and must begin his adventure to control and protect his new found family and friends. I will say it is a nice debut. It is fast paced and to the point. Which I am always a fan of. It is also heavily ATLA inspired and I am loving the opportunity to jump into a similar world with fun and powerful characters all trying to move forward and discover themselves and their goals." – @theladyravens

"Golden Eyed Legend is the perfect book for a fantasy lover, and the perfect book if you don't know fantasy or are new to it. I love the world building and the characters arcs. Calida was my favorite! I love a strong willed woman! This book gave me Avatar the Last Airbender vibes in the best way! It was action packed and hard to put down as you wanted to continually know what happened next. For a debut novel, especially in fantasy, I can say this checks all the boxes, amazing world building, likeable characters,

great buildup and character arcs and an ability to keep you engaged from the very first chapter. If I had to use one word to describe this book it would be impactful, you feel something from every character and it adds to the story."
– @paristhebibliophile

"I really enjoyed reading this. It's not the typical genre I would normally read, but after reading this it's something I'm interested in reading more! I thought the description, the imagery, and the flow of the book was spectacular. It's very well written for a first time writer! I can't wait to read more from you in the future." – @cheyennetatikaaa

"The world building in the Golden Eyed Legend is intricate and intriguing. I found the magic system unique and an immediate draw. Instantly, I was curious about Jai's backstory and wanted to know more. If you're looking for the next epic fantasy read, this is it!" – @dmcancel
** @dmcancel is the author of *Blood & Sunlight* and *Shadows & Secrets*

Wind invigorates life. To breathe is to live.

You are the seekers of truth and are in pursuit of infinite wisdom.

Your mind is the seat of your power. Intelligence and creativity are limitless to you.

Achievement is your greatest honor.

There are none more adaptable than you.

The way of the Wind is the way of peace, for the wise do not hold grudges in their hearts.

When life brings you to a turbulent place, inhale, let go - you are the Master.

BREATH | MIND | TRUTH

Exalted Heavenly Universe,

Thank you for the irrevocable journey you've guided me through. It has been an honor to be the One Who Knew. I will never know what made you choose me, but I feel blessed to have been chosen. You already know the weight of this journey. I'm honored that you found me strong enough to be the undertaker. With your guidance, I have achieved many milestones for my people. Unfortunately, I brought them many grievances as well.

I pray that the good of my life has outweighed my blunders. I also pray for her. Exalted Heavens, make her wiser than me. By the grace of the stars, remove all obstacles from her vision. Let her eyes be clear always. Grant her powerful wings that create hurricanes in battle and add a gentle understanding to her ways. Let her voice not be a whisper, let it echo. Help her to find truth, knowledge, and understanding in whatever she seeks. Challenge her, so she will feel worthy. Let her learn the lessons of patience young, unlike myself. I have given my most honest attempt to correct all of my errors. There has been progress in many places, but not enough to relieve the world of this dark abyss that I have contributed to.

Glorious Heavens, give her the wisdom to learn what to do and the proper time to do it. Bless her with friendships across the nations, just like you blessed me. I pray that some of my friendships surpass this lifetime and extend into hers. I thank you for all of your gifts, your guidance, and your mercy. I send my prayers to my successor. Please give clear sight to her mind's eye. And while she stretches her sight to the future, give her friendships to watch her back with love, care, and commitment. You've graced me with your mighty blessings. I am grateful.

-Basir

CHAPTER 1

A young, gray-haired woman struggled to keep her grip on the reins of her massive-sized owl while a vicious headache plagued her. She could feel the throbbing pain pulsating through her head, making it hard to focus on anything else. The sun was shining vibrantly across the sky, but she couldn't bring herself to appreciate it. Instead, she closed her eyes, hoping that the darkness would somehow ease the ache. Her mind swirled in a sea of thoughts. She deeply regretted leaving Pyroc so soon. Aqila had dealt with this headache for hours now, and[SM1] it seemed to get worse with every passing moment. She felt the pressurized sensation shooting behind her silver eyes again.

"Ugh, I need to have a vision."

Every seer had a symptom preluding the sight. This usually lessened once their training was complete. In the past, some seers would briefly lose sight, hearing, or taste; others would go completely numb when the sight came. Aqila always got a terrible headache that eased once her vision began to form, but she tended to have partial hearing loss mid-vision—one of the reasons she was working extremely hard to complete her training. That . . . among other reasons.

She pulled twice on the reins of her dasher, signaling for Talon to fly faster. It was midday. Talon needed to rest, and Aqila had to get to the desert without being seen by any other Landkeeper. The desert dunes of Theyra came into sight rather quickly. As they grew in size, Aqila shook her head a bit. She felt this vision coming on the horizon yesterday, and now it was ready to be seen. Intense shooting pressure was unusual except for the worst of visions. She'd only had a headache this severe one other time. This deeply troubled her.

In the desert of Theyra, where the sun blazed down with unforgiving heat, there were scattered several mud homes, standing low against the harsh environment. The homes seemed to rise out of the ground like ancient artifacts, as if they had always been there, baked by the sun and eroded by the wind. The homes were built of dried mud bricks, which had been formed by hand and then baked hard under the sun. The walls were thick, providing insulation from the extreme temperatures of the desert. The flat roofs were made of layers of woven palm fronds, which offered some shelter from the sun but not from the infrequent but torrential downpours that could flood the desert.

Despite their simple construction, the homes were carefully crafted with artistic flourishes. Each one was unique, with intricate patterns and designs carved into the walls or etched into the mud. Some of the homes had small windows carved into the walls, while others had decorative doors made of woven reeds or branches. Around the homes were scattered a few sparse trees, their roots stretching deep into the arid ground to find water. A few small animals scurried in the sandy soil, seeking shade or sustenance.

In the distance, the dunes of the desert stretched out as far as the eye could see, their smooth curves changing color as the sun moved across the sky. The wind blew constantly, carrying with it the fine grains of sand that settled over everything and slowly covering the mud homes like a blanket. Despite the inhospitable environment, the homes stood firm, a testament to the Landkeepers who had built them.

As the mud houses of the sparsely populated desert town came closer into view, Aqila landed Talon, her loyal Great Gray, with extreme ease. Despite being a Windmaster, she was safe in this part of Theyra. Talon stayed a few paces behind her as she set eyes on the library. It was a one-story building that stretched far left and right.

"All right, Talon, stay here until I come back—but if you need to hunt, feel free." The bird squawked as if he understood his rider. She reached into the carrying bag placed across Talon's body and carefully stacked seven books. The door of the library was a thick, hunter-green piece of fabric. Aqila pulled at the curtain and let herself in.

"Good afternoon," she called out in her usual slightly raspy voice. The dimly lit library created a unique, cozy ambiance. Bookshelves filled to the brim stood everywhere. The smell of paper and ink delighted Aqila's nostrils. It was easy to get lost in such a plethora of information. There were stacks of scrolls to her left and charts to her right. Aqila slowly continued inside, unsure if her friend and his family were busy.

She continued to walk through the modest house, once a hub of knowledge and learning. In one corner, a small nook, complete with a comfortable armchair and a lamp for reading, was tucked away from the rest of the room, offering a quiet and private spot to curl up with a good book. The walls were lined with floor-to-ceiling shelves, which had once been filled with books. The shelves themselves were a rich mahogany, and their intricate carvings and detailed molding spoke to the craftsmanship of the Landkeepers who built them. The scent of old books still lingered in the air, now mixed with the aroma of freshly brewed coffee.

"It's about time. I was about to dock you for being late. That would have been unfortunate for your flawless record," a deep voice boomed from behind her.

Aqila laughed, "Am I ever late, Bo?" She turned around to see her not-so-tall friend holding a clay mug filled to the brim with coffee.

"Don't give me that look just because you're a few inches taller than me," the Landkeeper raised his dark brown eyebrows as he brought the cup to his lips.

"I am more than just a mere few inches taller than you, just saying." Aqila placed her hand over her seven books. The Landkeeper nodded and walked behind a large desk off to one side of the room. As she gently set them on the desk, his sage green eyes focused on recording the books Aqila returned.

"Were they good reads, young scholar?"

"Of course, they were. I don't think your family can have a horrible book here," Aqila replied as she walked around the library. Her eyes were scanning the spines for a new read.

"So you say. You haven't had to log in the recent poetry collections in the romance category. Complete garbage if you ask me," Boaz replied, rolling his hooded eyes. He wasn't very tall, not even reaching six feet. However, Boaz was very broad and burly-shouldered as well as naturally muscular. His fawn, brown skin complemented his dark brown hair, which was short with gentle waves. He carefully observed his longtime friend before saying, "If you need to have a vision, feel free. No one else is here besides my parents. They are in the record room, and my siblings are at school."

"Thanks," Aqila replied almost absent-mindedly.

"What's wrong?"

"This vision! I need to have it, but I don't want to have it. I think it's a death vision, and I've had a death vision one other time before. They are incredibly painful and awfully vivid. I've been trying to calm myself and be at peace, so the images will come. Instead, I have a terrible headache that won't ease," Aqila stopped at a book as she spoke.

"Well, my friend, I can't help you in that department. However, I believe in your ability as an apprentice seer. Wait, that book's not up your alley. Try this, *Sign of Fire*. It's a good mystery," Boaz walked over and handed her the book.

Aqila laughed, "*Sign of Fire*? I don't believe in coincidences."

"I didn't say that you did," Boaz was confused by her remark.

She smiled, "Fire, huh? You're hardly going to believe this, I met the Golden-Eyed Legend a couple of days ago in Pyroc."

Boaz raised his short, thick eyebrows, "Really now? The Fireheart Legend? Isn't that something?"

"It was. His name is Jai, and he has the trademark golden eyes— the famed symbol of the rebirth of four great Legends. They were surprisingly gentle, though—" she abruptly stopped to massage her temples. "That's not good. The headache worsened when I thought about Jai. The death vision could be about him! I have to try and see this vision," Aqila became frustrated.

"Okay, okay, remember you told me that when you force it, sometimes the vision goes away completely. You don't want that. Do you know where the Legend was going?" Boaz asked.

"Not really. I gave Sheraga a message about Agni wanting to fight Pyroc, and I told him and Jai the location of Agni's headquarters. But Sheraga will meet with Tora, and I saw that in a vision last week. But nothing about Jai. Wait! I feel it," Aqila slowly turned her head and went outside.

CHAPTER 2

"Wow, that was a lot. Hope everything's going to be okay. Aqila's on it, everything will be fine," Boaz assured himself, taking a deep breath. His vision darkened until he could no longer see the library. It was a blank space, yet an ethereal calmness claimed him. His vision was shrouded in complete darkness for several moments. Suddenly, an image of a Landkeeper woman with fair skin, moss green eyes, and tiny freckles along the bridge of her nose appeared before him, saying, "It's almost time." Then she disappeared. His vision returned to him; he had never left the library.

"Ugh, I really don't like it when they do that. Almost time for what?" Boaz pondered over the woman's statement. He could not figure out exactly what she meant. The woman reappeared before him nearly transparent as he went back to grab the books Aqila returned.

"The world will know soon."

Boaz turned to the golden brown-skinned woman. "Ila, the world will know what soon? What is it almost time for?" Ila never moved. The ghost of her slowly disappeared. Boaz, still puzzled, proceeded to put the books away on their respective shelves.

*****

Outside, Aqila walked hastily away from the library. She didn't like having visions near the mud homes. Although this part of the desert was not heavily populated, it did not change the fact that she was still a Windmaster in Landkeeper territory. One wrong move could plunge the two races back into war. As her people's next seer, Aqila could not afford to be that careless. Struggling to see what was right in front of her, Aqila stumbled across the hot sand, her feet sinking deep into the scorching grains with every step. The leather of her flat shoes burned her feet. Sweat dripped down her forehead, and her breath came in short, ragged gasps as she pushed on through the unforgiving desert.

The sun beat down mercilessly upon her, casting harsh heat across her face and arms. Her skin glistened with a sheen of perspiration, and her loose clothes began to cling to her body, drenched with sweat. With each gust of hot wind, the sand stung her face and whipped around her in a frenzied dance. She gritted her teeth and pushed herself forward with sheer determination.

As she stumbled forward, her gray hair fell in limp strands around her face. Her silver eyes were fixed straight ahead, focusing on nothing but the dunes in front of her. Aqila kept moving, her feet pounding against the sand. She continued for nearly twenty minutes until the dunes bordering Ember were right before her.

"I think I'm far enough." Her vision became spotted. She took a deep breath, "This is for Jai," she said aloud. She began to focus on the areas where the pressure was stemming from. The sight was calling her, the sensation taking over her.

Aqila was a great distance from the library. She sat straight up on the fiery sand, legs folded. Her hands were gently lying on her knees, her palms open and upward facing. She focused on her breathing, allowing the sight to claim her. As she breathed deeper, the images she asked for finally appeared.

Her eyes glowed white as she became one with the sight. She saw Jai, Arrow, and their friends, the Flamethrowers. They were all at Agni's headquarters. There was an attack! They were fighting with Agni's soldiers! Aqila saw a fork in her vision. One fork, they all escaped safely, taking refuge in the desert. She saw rich brown skin, a man. He had hazel eyes. It was Tora! They took refuge with Tora! The images changed. In the second part of the fork, people died. Aqila searched the images for Jai. She saw the death of people she could not recognize. Then she saw Sheraga and Jai, followed by blood. A long trail of blood. Her vision violently spliced!

Aqila opened her silver eyes. Her heart skipped a beat. Her ears were ringing. Then there was a shooting pain in her neck. Her head felt like it was spinning. It was like she had been swallowed by a sandy dune. She couldn't focus. Her voice— she couldn't speak, and her body began to go numb. The desert grew fuzzy, then gray, then nothing at all.

Small chestnut complexioned hands pulled Aqila's long body onto the back of an oversized cat. Its fur was spotted with multiple shades of gray and black and patches of white that resembled flecks of freshly fallen snow, a snow leopard. The cat was massive. Its piercing bright blue eyes could gaze straight through someone's soul. Sleek, long black hair became tangled around Aqila as a young lady mounted the snow leopard.

"Ugh, this girl is a giant. Whatever. She knows who the Legend is, and that's all I need," her voice spoke softly. Standing at barely five feet tall, she couldn't lift the Windmaster. The snow leopard kneeled so its master could shove Aqila onto its back. It slowly stood as the young lady struggled to fasten Aqila onto its back. Highly irritated in the desert heat, the big cat began to yowl and chuff.

"Calm down, Mika. The sooner I tie her on, the sooner we can leave," she cooed in the cat's ear. Mika stilled, following the instructions of her owner. She tied Aqila up and mounted the snow leopard. "Good girl, Mika. Let's go!" The young lady turned back, her dark blue eyes looking around to see if anyone saw her, but no one was in sight. As the sun beat down mercilessly on the sandy desert, she gently petted the neck of her majestic cat, urging her to make way through the endless dunes. The snow leopard moved with a powerful grace, its muscular legs propelling it across the desert sands in long, effortless strides. The big cat carried its rider with Aqila fastened against her will and continued to quickly run away from the desert dunes.

At the library, Boaz was peacefully working away. He was organizing his parents' bills when he heard Talon squawking. "That's unusual," Boaz peeked outside and saw the Great Gray Owl puffing himself up in irritation. He walked toward it, but it became aggressive. Aqila didn't tie him down. If he was hungry, the bird could have hunted for himself. Boaz shrugged it off and went back inside. As soon as he sat down his vision darkened again and a tall man with long white hair appeared and whispered, "She's gone."

"Who? Aqila? She's outside. You know, having one of her visions," Boaz replied to the tall gray-eyed man. He turned away from him only for the man to appear again. "She's gone," he repeated.

After his vision was restored, Boaz walked outside. He passed the raging owl and continued into the desert. He had never received a message like that before. His stomach began to knot. Talon was trained to strictly obey Aqila's command. If he wasn't hungry, something else had to be wrong.

He knew Aqila would never sit near the mud houses to have a vision. She had a habit of walking until she could see the dunes on the border of Theyra and Lower Ember. He walked barefoot through the scorching sand, enjoying every moment. He loved walking through the desert on a hot sunny day like today. Boaz reflected on the meanings of the two wispy figures that met him in the blank space. It wasn't an unusual occurrence, but their messages were alarming. He walked to her usual spot, but she wasn't there.

"Aqila! You okay?" There was no answer.

If she's in the middle of a vision, she won't answer. Her senses are a bit impaired when sight comes to her. So she wouldn't answer.

Boaz shook his head and turned around. It had only been perhaps twenty minutes since he last saw her. She was probably fine. He turned on his heels only to return to the blank space and see the gray-eyed man again, "She's gone." Boaz's heart began to race. Quickly, he looked again. There was an imprint where someone had been sitting. Then the imprint of something else. The wind was picking up and the sand began to scatter.

Boaz swallowed hard, "Sh-She's gone." He ran back to the library, kicking up sand in his wake.

"Aqila!" He pulled the green curtain as he entered. A middle-aged, sage-eyed man appeared from the back of the library. "Okay, you better not say she's gone. I get the point now!"

"Bo, what's wrong?"

"I'm sorry, I confused you for someone else."

"Are you seeing things again?"

"I'm never seeing things . . . you know what, that's for another day. Dad, have you seen Aqila?" Boaz asked.

His father rubbed the back of his bald head with a mellow brown, veiny hand, "I heard her come in, but I haven't seen her at all. Maybe she left already."

Boaz shook his head, "She wouldn't have left without Talon. He's outside." Boaz's heart began to sink. Aqila was gone. His hands started to tremble, "She's gone. Something happened to her. Something happened to her. Something bad happened."

"Bo! Calm down!"

"I can't calm down! She's just disappeared on our turf!" Slowly walking to his father, he said, "I have to go. I have to get help. Aqila was speaking of having an important vision about—"

"Bo, no!" His father, equal in height and breadth, grabbed his son's shoulders, "Listen to me, whatever she told you, tell no other Landkeeper! You're right, you have to go. Go to the Windmasters and meet them head-on. We don't want to start another war. Tell them everything you know. If she dies, the cycle of seers, . . . This moment right here, what you do right now, will bring peace or war. I'll tell your mother. You go."

"I probably should take some things with me, I don't know what might come up," Boaz's mind was fragmented and scattered. He was running in circles aimlessly through the library.

I have to focus!

His father hurriedly grabbed a bag from one of the bookshelves and started filling it. "Get some extra clothes, and I'll get some food." The pair scurried around the library until the sack was semi-filled.

"Thanks, Dad," Boaz touched his father's shoulder before rushing out the door. When he looked at Talon, the owl began to squawk relentlessly. "Talon, take it easy. Aqila will be back soon, I promise."

He ran to the back of the library and set up his sand raft— a large plank of wood attached to a mast with a cloth to catch the wind. The edge curled slightly likened to a boat. He tied his sack onto the lowest part of the mast. Boaz led his raft to the front of the library. The wind was still today, but luckily for Boaz, the Universe gifted him in abundance. "No wind, huh? Well, sand ability will have to make due; thank you, Heavens," Boaz praised as he mounted his raft.

He spread his fingers and leaned his body weight forward. The motion of his hands began to pull the sand behind him. The raft moved faster as he gained momentum. If he kept up this pace, Boaz knew that he could reach the border of Kashmala in two hours. And for the sake of peace, he didn't have much choice.

CHAPTER 3

Aqila's eyes fluttered open. However, her vision was hazy. The spotted fur of the leopard caused her vision to swirl as if she had been running in dizzying circles. All of her limbs either felt heavy or numb. There was a searing pain in her head. Her blood felt like it had been set on fire, and she was sweating profusely. She tried to move her body to no avail. There was a pulsing pain in the left side of her neck. The only sound she could hear was the thumping of her rapid heartbeats.

Try to remember.

She kept thinking to herself. She recalled having a vision, a death vision, to be specific. There was a fork in the vision, meaning one small change in decisions could affect the entire outcome of the scenario. A feeling of dread wrapped around her like a blanket. She was attacked before she could probe further into who would make the pivotal decision and what it was about. Essentially, she didn't learn anything from the vision to help the situation. All she knew was the situation.

She was furious! As an apprentice seer, she must analyze the vision to gain an understanding of what she saw. Once she completed her training the meaning of the sight would come much quicker, but that power resided with her mentor, Zeroun, not her. All Aqila knew was that Jai was possibly in grave danger. She could feel nothing besides her fears and the slow churning of her thoughts. She just had to get her body to work.

Think, what have I been injected with?

Aqila realized that her attacker probably did not want her dead; this foreign substance was not intended to be poisonous or she would already be dead. Regardless, it was so strong. She took a deep breath and could feel her lips. They were dry, and when she focused hard enough, she could part them ever so slightly. Aqila pondered. Her whole body has been numbed, and now she can feel her lips?

Oxygen! She focused on breathing so much that her body was involuntarily producing extra oxygen for her respiratory system. The increase of oxygen was nullifying the foreign substance. Everyone knew that there were degrees of might. Some people had basic abilities, while others were gifted with incredible talents. Every Windmaster had a slight degree of control of oxygen, the foundation of their elemental power. The more one controlled their foundational element, the stronger they tended to be in general. Although she could manifest storms at will, Aqila did not have a great degree of control over oxygen. As a Storm, that usually was not problematic. Storms built their reputation on their ability to summon wild surges of power. She never needed to rely on the disciplined techniques required to master the base element. Unfortunately, her current situation rendered her unable to do anything. This caused her to be perplexed at the involuntary response of her body.

The good news is my body is fighting. The problem is I don't know how long I've been out. It could be days or weeks before I can naturally override this substance. I know Jai and Arrow don't have that long. The intensity of the vision means that the future is near. What I saw could happen later today or tomorrow. What can I do? I have to try to get the antidote. My attacker would have to have the antidote. Wouldn't they?

The more she thought to herself, the more her mind became clear. The negative, it was draining her to even think like this. Her eyes grew heavy, and her thoughts became muddled. The sense of clarity was only fleeting, the more she tried to concentrate, the more her mind seemed to rebel against her. Aqila forced herself to keep going, pushing through the mental fog enveloping her. But her efforts were in vain— her brain simply refused to cooperate any longer. She felt like she was wading through quicksand, her every thought slow and heavy. She took a deep breath.

If I can clear my mind, I can command my body to increase my oxygen level as if I were fighting. The increase would make me physically stronger. I may not make it out of here in time to help Jai and Arrow, but if I can get my vocal cords free, I'll be able to talk. If I can speak, I'll be able to get information and send it as well. I just hope he'll hear me.

CHAPTER 4

The dainty young woman adjusted her midnight blue fur cape over her shoulders. She looked back at the Windmaster lying motionless and patted her snow leopard's head as it purred. "Mika, I hope she's not dead back there. Maybe I shouldn't have given her the whole syringe full of that stuff. I don't know. Mika girl, take it easy as we go up the snowy mountains. The girl's tall, take it easy with the extra weight." Mika carefully pawed upward toward the top of a snow-capped mountain. They had been traveling all day and had almost reached their destination.

The massive snow leopard padded through the thickening snow, her powerful muscles rippling under her spotted pelt. She was a creature of grace and strength, moving with a fluid ease that belied her size. As she climbed higher up the snow-capped mountain, the air grew thinner and colder. But the leopard was built for this terrain— her large paws had evolved to grip the icy surface with ease. She moved slowly but steadily, each step calculated and deliberate. Mika was a creature of few sounds—the only noise was the soft crunching of snow under her massive paws.

"Good girl, we are almost there."

The big cat effortlessly pulled her rider and the captive Windmaster toward an icy mountain entrance. "Mika, stop here." The leopard immediately stopped in its tracks.

The blue-eyed young woman checked Aqila to ensure she was still appropriately fastened. She looked at Aqila's face, "Hope you wake up soon. You're no good to us sleeping." She looked up to see that it was beginning to snow. She went inside the mountain entrance, leaving Mika and Aqila outside.

"I'm back," she called in excitement. A young man appeared. Long, loose curls of dark brown hair contrasted his round, cerulean blue eyes. His mahogany-hued skin was cool and intensified the sharpness of his gaze. His chiseled jawline was peppered with freshly trimmed facial hair. The only delicate feature was his full lips.

This the pelt of a yak spread across the floor of the mountain cave. The walls were icy, and there were heaps of snow everywhere. The young man's tall, lean frame walked over, standing at least a foot over the girl, he peered into her eyes before asking, "Did you bring him?" He tapped his foot impatiently in his mink fur boots that stopped right underneath his knees, swallowing the bottom of his caribou skin pants. His parka was also mink fur. One could partially see his navy-dyed caribou skin shirt beneath the parka.

She pushed him back, "No, I didn't—"

"Then why are you back? What have you been doing the past few days?" He raised his voice.

"Will you let me finish? I didn't find him, I found someone who knows where he is, and I brought her instead. I think she'll be more useful. Come look! She's a baby seer."

"Tiber, are you kidding me? A baby seer? You brought a baby here?"

"Relax, she's not literally a baby. I had some business that Neptune wanted me to handle in Theyra. Yes, I know

I was supposed to go to Ember to look for Jai afterward. I was on my way, and I saw her having a vision. As she sat down, I heard her say something about Jai! The real seer is some old man, right? So this must be his apprentice!" Tiber's eyes beamed with excitement. She jumped up and down clapping.

"You know, many people have the same name, Tiber," the young man replied, his voice was smooth and void of emotion.

"Why would a Windmaster and a mini seer have visions about any old Fireheart. It was worth the capture," Tiber answered confidently.

"I don't think Neptune will be impressed with your reasoning."

"Nahal, I'll wait to hear that from Neptune himself," Tiber scoffed. "Help me bring her in, she's heavy."

Nahal walked outside to assist Tiber. He carefully eyed Aqila tied tight on the back of Mika. Her eyes were closed and her stray hairs were loosening from her braided crown bun. Tiber untied Aqila and Nahal lifted her effortlessly off the back of the snow leopard. Tiber rolled her eyes, "Show off."

"She's just tall, Tiber. Besides, how much of that stuff did you give her? Why is she out like this?" Nahal laid Aqila against an icy wall, and afterward, he tied her hands behind her back.

"The whole syringe," Tiber replied.

"What!" Nahal tied her ankles together. He placed his thin icy fingers along the pulse of her neck, "I'm shocked she's not dead. I told you that the stuff was made for hunting sharks and stuff. Does she look like a shark to you?"

"Sorry, I got carried away. The stuff just went in her neck so fast," Tiber put her hands up in defense.

"You idiot! In her neck? What made you do something so stupid? You were heavy-handed with the syringe," Nahal squared his jaw, "this could still kill her. You know that, right?"

"No! That can't happen! It was an accident! I thought you had the antidote," Tiber's eyes went wide.

"I don't! I never said I did! Neptune has it. And I don't think he's going to buy your ridiculous story. Leave it to the little girl to mess up a good plan," Nahal rolled his eyes.

"I am not a little girl. I am a woman!"

Nahal laughed insultingly, "Who can tell? You look like a child; you act like a child, so you're a child."

Tiber punched at Nahal. He swatted her hand away with ease, "You even punch like a twelve-year-old," he continued laughing.

"It's not funny," Tiber growled.

"Easy Tiber, I'm joking. It's not your fault your Changing hasn't happened yet." Nahal smirked. "Alright, all shards aside, I'll go to Neptune, and you stay with her and see if she talks."

"If she talks?"

"Yes, I was looking at the veins in her wrists. They are pretty large. It seems like her body is trying to increase her oxygen level. It will start from the head and proceed down. However, I'm afraid this will kill her before she can fully recover. You should talk to her once she comes around. She probably won't make it long, a day or so at best. She looks young, might even be around our age. An experienced seer would not be in this ridiculous situation and would have easily thwarted you. I heard when seers are apprentices they have some kind of weird response to having a vision, like passing out or going blind— weird stuff. But that goes away when they finish training. If she dies, an old seer will still be around for her people, can't be that big of a deal."

"I don't feel good about that. I didn't mean to hurt her. You are going to try to get the antidote, right?" Tiber looked worried.

"Of course I am! But if she dies, it's on you, the genius who shot her up with everything in the syringe. Good luck," Nahal calmly stated as he left the mountain. Tiber staggered and collapsed to the icy floor. She wasn't trying to kill anyone; it was a careless mistake.

She sighed, "Mika, come here, girl." The snow leopard bolted to her side. Tiber gently petted the top of the leopard's head. "I really messed up this time." Mika just purred.

Just as I thought, my body may expire before I completely free myself. I have to be careful.

Aqila had gained complete feeling throughout her entire head. She could see, hear, and smell properly. She was working on her vocal cords. Not being able to speak was testing her sanity. They were warming up but not quite ready for use. It felt like she had needles in her throat. The sensation felt like a fire had ignited in her mouth. She struggled to focus on increasing her oxygen level.

She didn't have the greatest control over it. But, in this situation, she didn't have a choice but to try. Tiber walked toward Aqila and peered into her face. Aqila opened her silver eyes and blinked at her.

"You're awake already. You must be quite gifted to awaken so soon. Nahal thought you could have died. Can you talk? Please talk!"

Aqila was silent. Her short, ragged breath was visible in the frigid air as she observed her surroundings. In the heart of an icy cave, deep within the recesses of a snowy mountain, her hands and ankles tied tightly, yet despite this, she couldn't help but be impressed by the cave's beauty. The walls were covered with glittering icicles that glistened in the dim light of the cave reflecting beautiful colors. The floor was covered in a layer of powdery snow. She was deep within the mountain, far from home, and completely at the mercy of Tiber and Nahal.

A snowy mountain? I must be in Avala - the Snow Tribe. Also, I know that I've been out for a few hours. In approximately three hours, I have gained feeling throughout most of my head. I just need my vocal cords to warm up some more. Then I can talk.

Aqila just blinked at Tiber. She had a childlike face. Based on her judgment, she did not appear to be much older than fourteen. Her body looked like a child's. Yet she had insisted that she was an adult moments before. Her voice was mature and didn't match her frame. Aqila began to feel dizzy, and she closed her eyes.

"Easy, Windmaster. Your body is increasing its oxygen levels, but it will wear you out. You need to rest. Try and talk to me if you can. Then I'll arrange to have you released."

Aqila became furious.

Have me released! I'm not an animal! I'm a seer and an esteemed citizen of Kashmala! I have to get the message to Jai and Arrow about the impending danger they're in . . . even if it kills me. I don't want to die, but if this is where my stars fade, the Universe knows best.

Aqila had hoped to live a full life, but she was determined to put her mission first. She had only done this technique a handful of times. She never needed it more than that. However, it was never at this distance. It was such an old technique that many of her people regarded it to be an old fable. Aqila knew from experience that it was not a fable at all. The technique had a strict requirement:

true love between two souls. She opened her mouth to talk, feverishly increasing her oxygen.

Tiber was just watching her. She saw the Windmaster's mouth open, "You're trying to talk. I'm listening!"

"What - do - you," Aqila huffed.

"What do I want? Tell me where the Legend is. You said his name, Jai! Tell me where Jai is," Tiber questioned. She sat on her knees close to Aqila, almost frantic for her to speak.

Aqila took a deep breath. She was tired, and her voice was almost ready. She closed her eyes and tried to recuperate some of her strength. Overriding her body's normal abilities was hard work.

Tiber eyed Aqila cautiously, she was sweating. This surprised Tiber, seeing that they were in a cold, snowy region. Sympathetically, she wiped the sweat from Aqila's forehead. "Well, while you try to gather some of your strength, I will introduce myself. My name is Tiber, daughter of Chief Dalit. You're in Avala. I need you to tell me where Jai is, and I'm going to tell Neptune, and you'll be released. It will be as easy as you make it," Tiber explained.

Hearing the word released while she was tied up only angered Aqila. The angrier she became, the more her oxygen increased.

Wait! When I'm mad, my oxygen increases naturally, just as if I were fighting. The more things happen naturally the more energy I'll conserve.

Aqila allowed her anger to fuel her oxygen increase. Her vocal cords began to feel ready for her to speak. "What do you want with Jai?"

Tiber was shocked at Aqila's testy tone.

"I don't want anything from him. But Neptune needs him. I don't know why. Honestly, I really don't know what's going on, or the big picture here. But Neptune is so powerful. He promised to save my people. Whatever he asks of me, I do. So where is Jai?"

"I don't know," Aqila replied, her body growing limp with exhaustion.

"Ugh, liar. Mika!"

The snow leopard went from lying quietly to standing alert. The majestic beast's thick fur glistened with snowflakes as it prowled through the icy cave. Its keen eyes locked on Aqila.

The snow leopard snarled, baring its razor-sharp teeth, its powerful muscles tensed, ready to pounce at any moment. Mika let out a deafening growl, as she charged toward the Windmaster, baring its teeth in Aqila's face.

Aqila didn't flinch but continued to speak, "I don't know. I was trying to have a vision before you rudely interrupted. Now, all of my senses have been impaired thanks to you. So when your Neptune arrives, I'll just let him know that you're the reason I don't know anything," she gasped for air. She had spoken too much.

Tiber's dark blue eyes went wide. She reflected on the events of the past few hours. The Windmaster was having a vision! Tiber *was* the reason the Windmaster didn't have the information. If Neptune heard that, her life would be on the line. Maybe if Nahal could get the antidote from Neptune, they could give her a little so the Windmaster could have her vision. If not, things would not be looking up for her.

After talking a little bit to Tiber, Aqila's vocal cords felt normal. Her entire face and neck felt normal. She could even turn her head ever so slightly. Now with a little focus, she was ready to calm her mind and prepare her message.

True love between two souls.

CHAPTER 5

Boaz could see the tall, vast Kashmalan mountains straight ahead. The mountain rock had been infused with flecks of metal, making them nearly impossible to topple. The mountain chain rose majestically from the earth, its peaks piercing the sky like jagged knives. The sheer size and grandeur of the range were awe-inspiring as far as the eye could see. They were a stunning blend of grays, with dark, rocky faces contrasting against the light blue sky. The metal flecks embedded within the rock glinted and shimmered in the sunlight like jewels. These flecks were of various sizes, some as small as sand grains, while others were as large as boulders. The beautiful silvery mix sparkled like stars in the night sky.

Despite their beauty, the mountains were still treacherous and dangerous, with steep slopes and deep valleys.

"Ila, you worked wonders on these mountains," he said. The ride across the desert was more difficult than he had anticipated. It was hard to maintain his speed over a long period of time. It took him more than two hours to arrive.

He looked around but saw no one. "Where is everybody?" He asked out loud. He thought the Kashmalan mountains were guarded by an elite group of fighters. Boaz questioned that as he stopped his raft. He dismounted after grabbing his sack and cautiously walked closer to the mountains. He could not shake the uneasy feeling that he was getting. Landkeepers and Windmasters are fifty years removed from a war that the Windmasters won. Coming this close to the mountains could be seen as an act of aggression. Boaz knew he had to keep going. He had to help Aqila however he could.

Boaz gently placed his fawn brown hand on the cool, semi-metallic gray stone mountain. He felt a harsh gust of wind overhead. When he looked up, something was diving toward him. He was tackled to the ground instantly before responding to what he saw coming toward him. He rolled for a bit in the sand from the impact. Boaz coughed up sand and tried to clear his throat as he staggered to his feet.

"State your business," a tall, limber man with heather gray eyes demanded. He was well over seven feet tall with dark, charcoal-colored hair that was short and very wavy. His skin was smooth, revealing his youth, and was a warm brown with rich golden undertones. "State your business," he repeated, louder as if Boaz did not hear him the first time.

Boaz realized that he hadn't prepared anything to say, "I need your help. Your seer is in danger!"

The Windmaster scoffed, "Do you expect me to believe that? Do you intend to divert my attention to spring an attack? Do you think I'm falling for it? The seer is at the top of the eastern mountains in the middle of training, as she should be. Look, if you don't want any trouble, just go back home," he turned away to leave.

"Aqila is in danger. She's not at the top of the mountain. She's missing, she came to the library to return some books, and she's missing. Doesn't that matter to you?"

The man stopped in his tracks. He turned his athletic body slowly, "So, something happened on your turf," his hand went for his circular blade, "right?"

This guy is impossible!

Boaz raised a sand slab to defend himself against the Windmaster. However, his attempt was futile. He jumped over the slab at an unbelievable speed before wind-kicking Boaz in the chest with a sweeping motion causing him to slide several feet back. Boaz staggered but remained standing, absorbing the blow.

"Stop! She's in danger! I came to get help, not to fight you!"

"But you admit, you allowed something to happen," the young man retorted. It was a fury of wind against the sand. Boaz could see that the Windmaster wasn't breaking a sweat, and he was utterly outmaneuvering him. He, on the other hand, was exerting a lot of energy, and most of his attacks just narrowly missed the tall master. Anything that managed to hit the Windmaster immediately was deflected as if he was wearing some sort of invisible armor. The gusts of wind and sand traveled upward. This was concerning for Boaz. He was struggling against one, and the sandstorm would only attract others.

"Look, just let me explain what happened," Boaz called to the Windmaster.

"Enough!" A loud voice called; it was deep like thunder. The dust and sand immediately ceased. As Boaz's vision became clear, he saw another Kashmalan Windmaster. Instead of wielding a circular blade, he carried a traditional sword sheathed on his hip. He was shorter than the other Windmaster by a few inches. His eyes were also heather gray but more piercing in his gaze. Their skin tones were similar. His shoulders were broader, and stone gray hair fell to the middle of his back.

"Kavi, I had everything under control," the taller Windmaster spoke.

"Really, Saar, everything's under control with a sandstorm running amuck? You. Can't. Do. That. The sand and dirt will continue upward straight into the state, and that's going to attract attention. Do you really want everyone to see their esteemed Wind Guardian tussling with a Landkeeper? Are you trying to start a war?"

"No, but in my defense, he approached the mountain and was touching it. I just came down, maybe a little too enthusiastically, and started asking questions. He was just trying to feed me a bunch of nonsense," Saar spoke.

"I was doing some important research nearby, but my concentration was broken listening to your ruckus,"

"But nobody told you to be listening," Saar muttered.

Clearly annoyed, Kavi turned to Boaz, "Landkeeper, what's your business?"

"I already asked that," Saar blurted.

"Are you a Landkeeper?"

"Heck no!"

"Then stop talking."

Saar's jaw dropped, offended at Kavi's response.

The way Kavi lowered his voice made Boaz feel uneasy. "I'm Boaz of Theyra. Aqila, your seer, is missing. Something happened to her. She came to the library to return some books, then she needed to have a vision, and she disappeared. She left Talon at the library entrance."

"Kavi, it's a ruse. We know it's a ruse! Aqila missing, we know better than that! Go do your job and leave me to do mine. I'll shoo him away," Saar groaned.

"If father were here, I don't think he'd see this as you doing your job," Kavi flatly stated. Saar rolled his eyes. Judging from their interactions, Boaz noted the pair seemed close.

"Besides, he's not lying," Kavi continued. Boaz shook his head, amazed that Kavi believed him.

"What! Well, you'd know. As you wish, I'm resuming my post," Saar acknowledged Kavi before turning toward the mountain. Saar expertly climbed up the mountain with extreme ease and agility. Within seconds, he was near the top.

Boaz was in awe at the sheer strength and agility of the Wind Guardian. "Forgive my brother. He can be on the impulsive side. The ruckus and your little sandstorm distracted me from my research. Come with me," Kavi whistled. Suddenly a large bird dove from the sky and perched beside him.

"That's the same kind of owl Aqila has! She calls her owl Talon," Boaz was excited to see something familiar that gave him hope for Aqila's safety.

"Quite correct," Kavi replied. He quickly positioned his foot onto the riding mat as he mounted. Boaz stood staring awkwardly. Kavi then motioned for Boaz to ride too. Boaz did not want to ride, but he could not scale the mountain like Saar, so this seemed his better option. He carefully climbed on top of Kavi's owl. He was not tall enough to put his foot in on the mat so he struggled to pull himself up. The owl shifted making it tricky to sit on the mat.

Kavi sighed, "Her name is Sterling. Don't fidget. It will make her uncomfortable."

Sterling slowly took off into the sky. Boaz didn't like the feeling of being in the air. However, he did not want to seem fearful in front of Kavi. He carefully observed the Windmaster. He wore dark gray harem pants. Similar to what Aqila usually wore. His long tunic came to his knees; predominantly blue and trimmed in dark gray and gold. His brother also wore the same dark gray pants, but his tunic was mainly white, covered in metallic silver mesh, and trimmed in dark gray. His tunic was also shorter, like the average shirt length. It was evident that Kavi's brother, Saar, was a warrior, and Kavi was not.

Sterling did not fly far; she landed near a cave in the middle of the mountain slope. Boaz was in awe of the little flecks of metal that glistened within the stone. Kavi dismounted with ease. Boaz slowly slid off, feeling rather uncomfortable with the heights. He looked around, and the cave appeared like a small study. There were papers and lamps everywhere. Fragments of plants and vials were scattered across the cave floor. Kavi calmly sat on a large rock near some of his papers. Crossing his long legs, he spoke, "All right, proceed. I can't take you into the city. But I'm intrigued to hear what you have to say. Especially if it involves Aqila."

"Like I said, she came to return books, and she needed to have a vision. She went outside and never came back," Boaz quickly spoke.

"You're going to have to do better than that," Kavi said in his low, deep voice. "What did she say? Be specific. I can't get a good picture without you being specific."

Boaz sighed, "She came to return some books that she had finished. I noticed that she seemed a little off—well, not quite like herself. I told her if she needed to have a vision, like she sometimes does, feel free to do so. She told me she needed a vision but could tell it would be a death vision. She said that she had had one before, and they weren't pleasant. Then she started talking about meeting the Legend. Yes, she met the Golden-Eyed Legend; his name is Jai. She was talking about him being in Pyroc, seeing Sheraga, and telling him that Agni was planning to go to war with him.

"Oh, then she said that she started to feel more pressure when talking about Jai and worried that the death vision was about him. Then she went outside, and I didn't see her again. She doesn't like to have visions near the library. She likes to get closer to the border, where she can view the dunes. After a while, Talon started to get really aggressive. He seemed so aggravated that I went to look for Aqila and couldn't find her."

Kavi went from looking calm, where Boaz couldn't tell what was on his mind, to looking furious. "So, you are telling me that my future wife went missing in your backyard?" Kavi walked toward Boaz slowly in a threatening manner.

"What! She's engaged to you?"

Kavi tilted his head, "We are to be married. Is there a problem with that?"

"Of course not! But Great Heavens, I didn't know that something was going to happen! She goes to have visions all the time," Boaz quickly started to explain.

Kavi turned around and sat down, "Did you tell anyone else these details?"

"No, only you."

"Good. Listen to me, Aqila is a powerful Windmaster, but she's quite vulnerable when the sight comes. It impairs her senses. Based on the information we currently have, the only thing anyone would want with Aqila without needing her to be a full seer would be to tell them where the Legend is located. I'll focus on finding her. You must ensure that the message gets to the Legend, regardless of circumstance. Aqila's future sight is short. What she sees in the future usually happens a few hours to a couple of days later. You have to get the message to the Legend. His life is at stake now. Don't worry about Aqila. I'll save her," Kavi instructed.

"How will I get the message to the Legend? I don't know where he is. Aqila mentioned that she told Sheraga and the Legend where Agni's headquarters was. Still, she didn't share the location with me—"

"Then you have to go to Sheraga," Saar entered.

"Although I didn't ask, thank you for your input, Saar. I was actually about to propose that. And before you ask, yes, I know where Sheraga is in real-time. He should be having an alliance meeting with Tora. The planned session should last a couple of weeks," Kavi informed.

"Come to think of it, she did say something about that briefly," Boaz murmured.

"Hey, I'm sorry I was so rough on you earlier," Saar acknowledged Boaz, patting his shoulder.

"It's fine. You were just doing your job," Boaz shrugged.

"Did you see anything when you went to look for Aqila in the desert?" Kavi asked.

"Um, nothing that stood out to me," Boaz admitted.

"Well, just keep talking," Kavi added, rolling his eyes.

"It wasn't much of what I saw. I thought I saw tracks for a moment, but by the time I got there and was looking for anything out of the ordinary the wind had picked up. I couldn't be sure. But now that we're talking about it, I did smell something," Boaz recalled.

"Blood," Saar interjected. Kavi glared at his brother, and the gaze was so intense that Saar dropped his head to avoid eye contact.

"No, it was something strange that I've never smelled before. Like an animal smell perhaps," Boaz couldn't put a name to something he had never smelled before.

"Well, this is enough for me to go after. Saar, do you think Hova could take Boaz to Tora?"

"I'll ask her, but she probably won't mind. I'll go to her now," Saar bolted out of the cave at lightning speed.

Kavi stood up and walked past Boaz. His long gray hair flowing behind him, "I know our people have not been on the best of terms, but thank you for letting me know about

Aqila. I'll ensure she knows that her Landkeeper friend was a valuable ally in her cause."

"Thanks, anything I can do to help, I'm willing to fight and do," Boaz replied genuinely.

"Your efforts are appreciated. I have to prepare to retrieve my fiancé. My brother will see you off." Kavi nodded to Boaz and proceeded to leave the cave. Immediately upon stepping outside, Sterling perched herself beside him. He gracefully mounted the giant Great Gray and rode her upward toward the State of Kashmala.

CHAPTER 6

Upon landing in the mountain state, Kavi sent Sterling off to hunt. The city was not too active because most children would have just returned home from school at this time. Kavi briskly walked into the Capitol, the large estate for Kashmala and Wyndhm's government. The elaborate estate sprawled across acres of lush greenery, its grandeur visible from miles away. The gray marble buildings rose high above the trees, gleaming in the sunlight. Each structure was a masterpiece in its own right, adorned with intricate carvings and towering spires. The center-most building was made of pale gray marble; that was where Kavi's family resided. The walls were made entirely of gray marble, giving it a regal and imposing appearance. The roof was adorned with ornate tiles, with a grand dome sitting atop the central pavilion. He briskly ran up the marble steps and inside the Capitol.

The interior walls of the Capitol were pale blue except for the wall behind the thrones of the rulers. That one was a gentle yellow. There were gold banners near all of the rooms' six-foot windows. The massive, long rug of the foyer was silver and trimmed in gold embroidery. The windows were tall and narrow, allowing streams of natural light to flood the interior. A man and woman who looked to be in their fifties occupied the thrones. The man had short, curly charcoal hair and steel-gray eyes. His golden brown skin gave no signs of aging. He wore dark gray pants and a long silver robe tunic. He was in deep conversation with the woman to his right. She was lovely. Her heather eyes had a curious twinkle dancing about them. Her skin was richer than her companions, while her long, straight waist-length hair was tamed in a high ponytail with a hairpin adorned with a youthful pink round stone dangling from the silver stem. Her light gray harem pants were barely visible underneath the floor-length baby pink tunic with silver and crystal closures.

As Kavi approached them, the pair ceased their conversation and turned their attention to him. Kavi bowed his head slightly, respecting the Rulers of Kashmala, "Father, Mother, good afternoon. I have come before you requesting an immediate leave of absence for a few days." Kavi looked his father directly in the eye.

"Immediate? Has something transpired?" his father asked, his voice low and calm.

"Something rather urgent has transpired. The urgency is such that time does not permit me to explain in great detail," Kavi replied.

Kavi's father eyed him intensely, "Leave of absence granted. You will resume all duties immediately upon your return."

"And you will have a counsel with us the evening of your return to inform us of your urgent business," his mother added, smiling gently.

"Of course, I wouldn't have it any other way," Kavi bowed. His parents nodded to him, the signal of dismissal. Kavi veered to the stairs left of the thrones. He jogged upstairs and walked past three bedrooms before arriving at his own. Kavi felt a presence behind him, "You know it is impossible to sneak up on me."

Saar was leaning on the door frame of Kavi's light gray bedroom, "I wasn't trying to sneak up on you. I just want to let you know that Hova will meet Boaz and me at the border. I didn't feel good about leaving him inside our territory. I just wanted to take all precautions." Saar noticed his brother taking his sword from his sheath, pouring a clear liquid onto a cloth, and wiping his blade with it. "Kavi, I'm not knocking your fighting skills, but are you sure you want to go alone?"

"Don't insult me," Kavi replied as he wiped his blade.

"No, don't get me wrong. You're a great fighter. You're not me, but you're still good. You're my toughest opponent since you're so smart. I mean, we're like equals! I-I- we have never not fought together. We're a team. I'm the Storm, and you're the man with the plan . . . that always works."

"That's right, you're the fighter, and I'm the thinker," Kavi murmured, giving attention to his blade.

"Wow, you admit I'm the stronger brother," Saar gasped playfully.

"I have never hidden nor denied the fact that you are physically the stronger brother, but we both know that you are also the dumber brother. Stay out of trouble while I'm gone," Kavi looked back at Saar, smirking.

Saar laughed, "I just wish I was going with you."

"I know. Those were the days, weren't they? Saar, things are different now, you're needed here. You're the leader of the WindGuard now, and being the Wind Guardian is a lot of responsibility."

"I mean it's not like I can never leave. Lujayn is the best First Guard, they would be just fine in her hands."

"The WindGuard is *your* responsibility—not hers. If I needed help, I'd ask. Brother, I'll be fine, and you know that. I may not be a Storm, but I'm still incredibly gifted. Someone was bold enough to attack Aqila, who is taller than the average man—"

"She's short when she sits, though," Saar interrupted.

"That is not the point," Kavi rubbed his eyebrows. "If they are bold enough to do that, they're bold enough to try us. While I'm gone, if anyone comes looking for her or asking about her, lock them up."

Saar met his brother's intense gaze, "I will," he vowed.

"I'm leaving for the Waterbearer Tribes. I—"

"Waterbearer Tribes? How do you know she's there?"

"Don't interrupt, then you'd know," Kavi snapped. "Boaz said he smelled an animal that was unfamiliar to him. Landkeepers come across all kinds of animals. There are only a few animals he would not have been able to recognize by scent. Most of them are in the cat family. Only Waterbearers habitually ride cats. Ninety percent of cat species in the world are found in Waterbearer territories. Theyra shares borders with every people except the Waterbearers. So it makes sense that he would not have known the smell. Boaz was honest about everything he said. He never lied. So my reasoning makes—" Kavi stopped mid-sentence and tilted his head left.

"Brother what's—" Saar stopped when Kavi put his hand up before his face, silencing Saar. Kavi continued to tilt his head, his eyes locked on his brothers. Minutes passed, and Kavi never changed his posture. Saar was beginning to get worried. Kavi had never had such a violent look in his eyes.

Kavi sighed and shook his head, "I know exactly where she is."

"Where?"

"The Snow Tribe!"

"Avala? How did she end up there?"

"Aqila just sent me a wind song. She said she was injected with something that left her paralyzed; she's increasing her oxygen level to override her body. Wait a minute. Great Heavens," Kavi turned around and started rummaging through the desk in the corner of his room.

"What are you looking for? Let me help you," Saar walked inside.

"It's all making sense now. Grab my letter box from my closet." Kavi pointed to the closet door.

Saar looked in the closet and groaned upon seeing several stacks of letter boxes, "Which one?"

"Red one in the shortest stack, it should be the one on the top. The first letter in the box is the relevant one." Kavi continued to look through several vials in his desk drawers.

"How in the raging winds do you keep up with all of this?" Saar muttered as he spun around, nearly lost in letterboxes. Minutes later, he retrieved the right one.

"This one from Chiefess Marina of the Beach Tribe," Saar started to skim the letter, "it's talking about not receiving the whale tranquilizer. What does that have to do with anything?"

"I sent that to her a month ago, and she says she never received it. I returned a letter telling her I would make some more and deliver it myself. The symptom of the whale tranquilizer would completely paralyze a person and eventually kill them if they did not receive the antidote, which I am looking for."

"Why did you make something like that?" Saar raised his eyebrows in disbelief.

"It wasn't supposed to be used on a person! I specifically labeled it, saying to use it with caution and explaining that it would paralyze a human. I specified that it should only be used on sharks and whales because they're so large that it would just put them to sleep. Aqila's symptoms align with my research on the tranquilizers' effect on the human body. Her body will increase the oxygen levels, relieving some of the paralysis. However, the compound is so strong it will still kill her if I don't give her the antidote. I'm just furious. Someone used the fruits of my research to harm my fiancé," Kavi growled as he reached into the back of his desk drawer. He slowly grabbed a vial with a golden liquid, "Got it!'

"You got the antidote? That's great. But if you go to Avala and attack, it could start a war with the Snow Tribe right along our borders." Saar's heather-gray eyes widened with concern.

"And? Does it seem like I care? I love her! I'd wage war with every Nation if that's what it takes to protect her. Avala is already docked as the instigator if it comes to war. Avala has already initiated an act of war by kidnapping a seer. That's the equivalent of one of us kidnapping a Waterbearer chief. I will send such a message that will make them regret ever putting a hand on her. I may not be a warrior, but I, Kavi, heir to the Kashmalan throne, am not to be trifled with. Not a soul will stop me from protecting the woman I love."

"Take care, brother." Kavi and Saar shook hands.

The brothers parted ways, and Kavi whistled for his dasher. The pair both acknowledged their parents with a brief nod on the way to the Capitol doors. Sterling landed a few feet from her rider. Kavi mounted and slipped the antidote into the bag strapped to Sterling's right side. Saar watched his brother fly off westward in the direction of Avala.

"I've never seen him like that. Heavens be with him and Aqila," he whispered. He suddenly remembered that Boaz and Hova would be waiting for him at the border. With a sense of urgency, he hurried toward the border.

CHAPTER 7

Aqila regarded Tiber carefully. She seemed anxious. Her snow leopard Mika mirrored her rider's anxiety, her pelt standing straight up. The sound of her heartbeat crashed in her ears like thunder. Aqila wiggled her shoulders slightly. She could feel most of her arms, and her hands were beginning to tingle. After talking to Tiber earlier, she sent her wind song. She was hopeful that it would reach him. When she learned of the wind song years ago, Aqila was fascinated. After successfully learning the technique, she confirmed it was not a fable. However, the technique is only effective if the two souls who are attempting to communicate are truly in love, a marriage of souls. It was a stretch, but Aqila was hopeful that Kavi had received her wind song.

Aqila noticed Tiber's frustrations and decided it would be wise to see if she could extract information from her. Just as she thought of this, Nahal returned. Tiber jumped to her feet, "Did you get the antidote? She spoke a little bit. After she talks, she gets exhausted," Tiber explained.

"I went to his usual location, but he wasn't there. I asked around and learned that he had a meeting with Agni, and he won't be back for a couple of days," Nahal sighed.

Agni! Agni and Neptune know each other. How so?

"She'll probably die!" Tiber exclaimed, grabbing Nahal's parka and shaking him.

"And who's fault is that?" He swatted her hands away, "You're the one who went crazy with the stuff, and it's not my job to fix your mistakes." Nahal looked at Aqila, "But I must say, she's handling it well. She must be powerful. It's a shame such a pretty face has to suffer and die due to the carelessness of a little girl."

"Pretty? You know she's a Windmaster! And stop calling me a little girl," Tiber huffed.

"Obviously, she's a Windmaster. Chill, I'm not in love with her!" Nahal shrugged his shoulders, "Look, I really did try. What else do you want me to do? Neptune wasn't there."

Tiber started trembling. Nahal gently grabbed her shoulders, "Hey, listen to me. Just keep trying to talk to her. She might die, but as long as you get what Neptune wants, you won't be subject to his wrath. Even if she dies, it will be worth it, right? Our cause, our people, don't forget what we're fighting for. We're doing this for our tribe. If one person has to die to save our people who have been dying for hundreds of years, it's worth it. It's just one life."

Nahal looked around, "I have to go on my assignment. I'll come back tomorrow. If she's dead, I'll help you get rid of her body. The world will think she's missing and won't attach this to you. It will be okay. We're on the same team; it'll be okay." Nahal gently pulled Tiber toward his chest, hugging her. Tiber pulled away from him slowly, and Nahal hesitantly left her to tend to the Windmaster.

Seems like Tiber has a conscience, and Nahal doesn't. I should try to talk to her. If Neptune and Agni are working together, that could pose some problems.

The feeling in her hands was returning. It was not as difficult now that she had been increasing her oxygen. She hoped that things would not flip and make a turn for the worse for her.

She turned toward Tiber. "If I'm going to die tomorrow, you should give me an explanation as to why you're doing this," Aqila demanded.

"It was an accident. I didn't know that you'd be paralyzed like this. I just work for Neptune. I was doing a job, and I made a mistake," Tiber was shocked at Aqila's tone.

"You know the Universe punishes those who murder without reason," Aqila hissed.

"Don't say murder! I didn't mean to!"

"If I die because of this, my blood is on your hands. It's still murder. Like I said, the Universe has punishment for murder without reason."

Tiber scoffed, "The Universe? All the Universe ever does is punish and take. I can't believe people still believe in that fable."

"The Universal Order is not a fable but a set of laws to govern the world. What happened to make you disbelieve so strongly?"

"I've never been given a reason to believe in the first place! Look at me! I still look like a child. Who's at fault?

The Universe! My people suffer from scarcity of food and shelter. Who's at fault? The Universe! I'll never know the sound of my mother's voice because she gave her life to give me mine. Who's at fault?" tears slowly streamed down her face, "The Universe. I don't have a reason to believe, Windmaster. The Universe is the source of all of my pain and suffering."

"My name is Aqila. And nothing happens without reason! I'm sorry that you had to go through those things. But you're not the only person who knows pain and suffering. What about Ember, where so many fathers were killed in war and never returned to their families? What about their children? What of their wives who gave birth to babies that would never know their fathers? What about the children in Theyra living through a civil war who don't know where their next meal is coming from or if they will die tomorrow? What about what you've done to me?! My parents gave me up so I could fulfill my destiny as a seer, and I have to sit here, slowly dying, and the only thing you have to say to me is that you made a mistake!"

"What do you have to say now? I never met either of my parents! I don't even know their names. My mentor is almost three hundred years old, and my death would have wasted the last ten years of his life. If I die, the cycle of the seers will be broken and a part of my people's history and identity fragmented. I'm sitting here while my destiny, legacy, family, and the man I love—people I'm supposed to serve—are slipping away from me . . . and I haven't turned my back on the Universe yet. You don't have an excuse!"

Tiber stood on her two feet, perfectly healthy. She wiped the tears from her face. Her heart was hurting. This woman was dying in front of her and had so much faith. So much faith while knowing that she was going to die. "I-I'm sorry, Aqila. I didn't mean . . . I just wanted to save my people. I'm tired of this curse the Snow Tribe suffers from. None of us Snow Tribe children ever knew our mothers. The moment we were born, they died. It's been like that for two hundred years now. My father is the chief of this tribe. His first wife died when my older sister, Shasa, was born. Father raised her by himself." Tiber walked over to Aqila and sat beside her.

"Then he married my mother. She was from the Jungle Tribe. She, too, died right after I was born. My sister helped my father raise me. She's like my mother. I just can't imagine how wonderful life would have been for both of us if fate had not claimed our mothers.

"Now my sister's married to Nahal's brother, Muraco. They've been married for three years, and now she has only five months before fate claims her. Neptune promised that he would reverse the curse on our tribe if I served him. Aqila, you have to understand. I'm just serving him so my sister won't have to die." Tiber sobbed into Aqila's shoulder.

A part of Aqila felt terrible for Tiber. Still, it was not the Universe's fault. "I am sorry that you experienced this. I know you love your family and your tribe. I love my family and people too. But the Universe punishes us when we have erred and then turned away. However, when you repent with a true heart, the Universe also forgives. We shouldn't look for others to liberate us when we can liberate ourselves if we really tried."

Tiber sat up and shook her head, "I just … don't believe that."

"I know you don't believe it, but the truth doesn't change because one chooses not to believe in it." Aqila raised her eyebrow.

Tiber looked down at her hands. She had a strong urge to free Aqila though she didn't have the antidote. The urge to stop and set her free pulsed through Tiber's mind. She decided to try and get Aqila to speak comfortably.

"I heard that your people were born from the wind. Is that true?"

"Yes, in the first year, after the brothers of fire walked the earth, the brothers of wind were born. After the twelve stars fell and transformed into people bringing the heavenly revelations, the brothers each married one of the twelve stars. The oldest brother's family became the Blue Clan of the North, the second became the Green Clan of the South, and the youngest became the Yellow Clan of the East. They lived in peace and harmony embracing their natural talents for thousands of years.

"The Blue Clan was known for wisdom and learning, the Green Clan was known for agriculture and nature, and the Yellow Clan was known for creativity and innovation. In time, members of each clan broke away to the West to start the Red Clan, rebellion settled in their hearts, altering their nature. That clan became known for fighting and war.

"The Red Clan was difficult to live with in peace most of the time. However, whenever the Windmasters were threatened, the four clans joined forces showcasing their variety of talents. Eventually, the first seer saw a prophecy that required the four clans to become one. And from that prophecy, the Windmaster territories eventually became the sister states of Kashmala and Wyndhm."

"I wish I knew more about the Waterbearer's origin story." Tiber sighed, she didn't want Aqila to die. She decided to free her as soon as she gave up Jai's location. "Aqila, what is it like to be a seer?"

"A lot of pressure— a seer is not even born once every one hundred years. So to be chosen for such a unique destiny is truly an honor. My mentor, Zeroun, took me in at ten to begin my training. It was a lot of reading and learning how to read visions. They come like images flashing before my eyes. Sometimes it's clear, and sometimes it's blurry. Sometimes you can hear what's going to happen. But to handle the sight takes a lot of work and a lot of patience and discipline.

"Sometimes you have to sit for an hour to get fifteen minutes worth of images. It's really a skill and an art. Zeroun navigated me through it all. I never met my parents, but Zeroun has been a father to me. He taught me so much. Not just about becoming a seer, but about cooking, gardening, and even how to take care of my pet.

Our favorite thing to do together was go outside with our telescopes and watch the stars.

"If I wasn't to be a seer, I would have further pursued astronomy in school. Zeroun really nurtured me and loved me. I just can't imagine a world without him. I feel like I really let him down. He waited so long to have a student for this to be my end." Tears started to fill Aqila's eyes at the thought of never seeing her beloved mentor again. She noticed that she could move her chest and stomach freely. Aqila was secretly thrilled. She observed how moved Tiber seemed to be hearing about her life as a Windmaster.

I have to keep this up. I need her to let her guard down.

Aqila slowly began to try to twist her wrists in her rope bondage. She knew she couldn't move too much. She had to keep Tiber believing that she was ready to die.

For some reason, my body is not feeling as tired as before. Maybe because I'm a Storm, I can fight this substance a little more. Everyone is so convinced that I should be dying. I'm in pain, but the extra oxygen is helping me. I still need to be careful. It's the evening, and I can't feel anything below my navel.

Aqila was planning her next moves carefully as Tiber rose and walked back to Mika, who was sleeping peacefully.

"Have you met the Legend in person or only in visions?"

"I have had a few visions, and that's how I knew his name," Aqila lied.

"Do you know where he's going or where he currently is?"

"No, I've seen his face and heard his voice in visions, and I had a vision about him before you attacked me. Now, I'm sitting here paralyzed and can't have any visions at all," Aqila grumbled.

"What do you remember about Jai?" Tiber persisted as she picked the skin on her fingers.

"His trademark golden eyes . . . besides that, everything is fuzzy," Aqila replied calmly. Tiber sighed. Aqila sensed that she was getting frustrated. It was true, Aqila could not have any visions at the moment, but her memory was working just fine. She decided to probe Tiber's frustrations a little more, hoping she would reconsider. "You seem to put a lot of trust and faith in Neptune. Did he ever tell you how he would free your tribe from the curse?"

Tiber tilted her head at Aqila's question, "No, he didn't."

"Well, if you don't believe in the Universe, you must not believe that Neptune is a Legend himself or anything. Actually, since you don't believe in the Universe, why do you even think that Jai is a Legend?"

"Neptune is very powerful, and I've seen him do incredible things. He is working so hard to make things better in Avala! He's in a league of his own, and he doesn't have to explain himself to anyone," Tiber defended her leader.

"Really. But if you don't believe in the Universe, where does Neptune generate such power? Why do Legends exist? Why do you even believe that the concept of a Legend is possible?"

Tiber was getting frustrated with Aqila's questions, and she didn't have the answers to them. Water flowed from her fingertips, and in sheer anger, she threw a freezing cold water ball at Aqila's face, "Shut up! Stop asking me questions like that!" Mika growled, mirroring her owner's anger.

"Ugh, I was just asking. Who knew you'd get mad because you know that there are things about Neptune that don't make sense," Aqila spat, cold water dripping down her face and onto her shirt.

"What did you say?" Tiber glared at Aqila.

"Well, if Neptune is your leader, you should be prepared to answer people's questions about his credibility. But it seems you can't do that. You say you don't believe in the Universe, but you don't know where his power comes from. You say that you're doing these criminal things, kidnapping and poisoning people, in exchange for favors from Neptune. However, you don't know how he plans on keeping his end of the deal. So if you don't know that, how can you be sure that he's not lying to you? Regardless of how you feel, the truth is that if you don't have those answers, you can't prove to anyone that he's not lying, not even to yourself."

"Neptune wouldn't lie to us. He's one of us. He lost his wife and child, and then he vowed that he would break the curse for the rest of us," Tiber spoke, convinced.

"Okay, so what about the rest of your folk who believe in him? What about all the other favors that have been done for Neptune? And after all of this, new mothers are still dying? Tiber, do better. I'm not convinced."

"You know what? You don't have to be convinced! You're not one of us. You're not a Waterbearer, much less a part of my tribe. You're not suffering what we suffer. It's not for you to understand."

Aqila smirked, "So you say. You don't believe in the Universe, yet I gave you a clear explanation for everything I am. I don't believe in Neptune, and you're not giving me a reason to believe that he's not a lying phony! Go ahead, Tiber! Argue back. You're just going to get mad when I ask you to prove it!"

Tiber was furious with Aqila. She felt the water come to her fingertips again. She repeatedly threw water at Aqila until she was thoroughly drenched, coughing up water, "You—shut up!" Tiber rode Mika out of the icy cave.

Aqila shook her head. Water droplets were flying everywhere. "I'm finally alone." She took a deep breath. She had been turning her wrists for several minutes. By keeping Tiber worked up and frustrated, she never even noticed. The rope around her wrists was loose enough to free one hand. Aqila knew that all she needed was to free one hand. She was paralyzed from the naval down, but overall she didn't feel too bad. She still wanted to be careful that she did not jeopardize her health by trying to get away. Her mind concentrated on Jai. She hoped that he was okay. "Glorious Universe, please be with Jai. No one knows destiny better than you," she praised the Universe.

Now that Tiber was gone, the weight of everything that had happened was hitting Aqila hard. She was paralyzed from the waist down. Her abilities were compromised by a foreign substance. She had promised Jai that if she had a vision, she would alert him, but now his life was at risk, and she couldn't get anywhere. Her mentor depended on her to finish her training and become a full seer. If she died here, that wouldn't happen. Even worse, her death would break the cycle of seers, which had never happened, ever. She would fail as a seer and fail her people. She would never meet her parents who birthed her into such an incredible destiny. She would never marry the man she loved. She promised them that she would become a great seer. It was scary that she couldn't even see her own destiny. She sighed.

I don't want to die like this. I don't want to let my people down. If I focus on what I can do right now, I won't. The Universe knows what's best.

Aqila fought to boost her spirit. She sent a message to her fiancé already. He was a powerful Windmaster who could manipulate sound waves. His range of hearing was more extensive than the average Windmaster, who already can hear better than any other people on earth. She sent him a wind song, the closest thing to telepathy between two Windmasters who shared a deep intimate bond. The deeper the bond, the greater the range the message could travel. If the distance was not too great, there was no doubt in Aqila's mind that Kavi would come for her. They had much practice with the technique when she was away high in the eastern mountains training with her mentor. However, that was back when they both were in Kashmala. Never had either of them attempted it at such distance. This would be a test.

As much as she desired to be rescued, she didn't want to put Kavi in danger either. The thought of someone injecting him with this was enough to send her into a spiraling emotional abyss. Aqila took a deep breath.

Trust it. Trust him. Kavi is as intelligent as he is powerful. If it works, he'll be here. If not, I will keep fighting.

She closed her eyes, intensifying the memory of him. Kavi's proficiency with sound was a force to be reckoned with in itself. He could tell if someone was lying by listening for sudden inconsistency in their heartbeats. She smiled at the thought of him. His memory gave her strength. Missing him gave her hope as well as deep regret. After having a sudden vision, she left before she had a moment to speak with him. "I hope the distance was not too far."

CHAPTER 8

Smoke filled the air mercilessly. A hazy veil obscured the battlefield from view. The smoke rose from the ruins of what had once been a thriving village, now nothing more than a scene of destruction and chaos. The buildings that had once stood tall and proud were reduced to rubble, their charred remains smoldering in the brutal battle. The acrid smell of burning wood and flesh filled the air, making it difficult to breathe. The smoke stung the eyes and coated the throat, leaving a bitter taste in one's mouth. The world seemed to have been transformed into a dark, surreal landscape.

The atmosphere was tainted with war and singed by fire. The border of Upper and Lower Ember was a battlefield. An air of uncertainty troubled Emberites from both sides. Not mentally ready for war, the people of Upper Ember stayed away from the border. Not physically prepared for war, the people of Lower Ember stayed away from the violent border.

As day turned to dusk, the Flamethrowers were pushed to their limits, severely outnumbered, and exhausted from battle. Cahya, Calida, Yuuna, and Beamer had successfully freed Sitara, and she swiftly left to resume her secret duty. This allowed four more Flamethrowers to engage in battle with Agni's minions.

Inside the headquarters, the Flamethrowers were in the thick of the battle, led by Arrow. His Pyrocean genes awakened in full force, making him outstanding in battle. Breathing fire and being of fire, anyone with eyes could see how blessed the family of the DragonLords were. His gifts were extraordinary. It was as if he had become a shapeshifter. His skin became a leathery dark gray, his teeth became fangs, and the oddly faint jade scales near his eyes glowed eerily as his short fingernails grew into claws. This is what it means to be Pyrocean, to be a Dragon. He traveled by fire to attack and returned to the side of his fellow Flamethrowers, watching and defending their backs like a true soldier. Suvan, gifted with superhuman strength and power, also protected his fellow Flamethrowers. His liquid flames hypnotized whoever was weak enough to be lured by their intimate dance, only to be dangerously beckoned to their deaths. The duo fought to defend their Legend as he confronted Agni.

The roof was on fire, and the left side of the stone castle roof had completely burned down. However, the Flamethrowers fought without fear, determined not to leave without imprinting their flames into the minds of their opponents. Arin and Kiran fought soldiers on the first floor. They were back-to-back, handling their own, to the disbelief and amazement of the enemy Firehearts, as the vast majority were not gifted in anything but hand-to-hand combat. Alena was pursuing Zay on the teetering roof, luring him away from Jai so he could confront Agni. The roof was burning quickly, as she was hot on his heels. When she closed the distance on him, she attacked with fiery punches. However, Zay's reflexes were acute. He blocked every punch with pinpoint accuracy, not phased by the threat of fire. His combat fighting was impressive, especially for one not gifted with the flame.

"Just give up already. It's almost night, and you're losing. Just give it up," Alena panted, struggling to breathe through the smoke.

"The only one who seems tired is you. Looks like you need to work on your stamina, Firefly," Zay replied.

"Firefly! How dare you!"

She continued her pursuit. They had been running, ducking, and dodging for nearly an hour, and he was not breaking a sweat. Alena was thankful that he wasn't a gifted Fireheart, or she would have been in serious trouble. Zay punched, then attempted to strike her with his elbow. Alena blocked the punch and narrowly dodged his elbow. However, the elbow was a diversion from the sweeping motion of his foot. Alena tripped and fell backward as the roof was already unstable under her feet. Her eyes went wide, and fear ran through her veins at the thought of falling from at least fifty feet in the air. Her heart raced as her wide, fear-filled eyes locked onto the inferno raging below.

Flames danced hungrily, clawing at the edges of the rooftop where she teetered. The acrid scent of smoke stung her nose, and the crackling roar of the fire drowned out everything else. Her breath hitched, chest heaving, at the realization that death was near. Every fiber of her being screamed for safety, and yet the precipice beckoned, her terror and the searing heat locking her in a harrowing dance. She closed her eyes awaiting a painful death.

A subtle wave of peace washed over her, she was not falling. A hand had tightly grasped her wrist. She dared to open her eyes. Looking up, she saw that Zay had grabbed her, "Pull yourself up!"

"No! Let me go," Alena spat.

"Don't be stupid. You want me to drop you into a burning pile of rubbish. You fall, you're gonna die. Pull up!"

"No, I'd rather die like this," Alena choked, trying not to cry.

"I'm not trying to kill you, Firefly. If I wanted to kill you, rest assured, I wouldn't be holding onto your life right now," Zay gently spoke. Unsure if she was too weak or too scared, he used his strength to pull her up from dangling on the edge of the burning roof. Never once did she grab onto him for safety. Could she really want to die?

After pulling her to somewhat of a safety zone, despite the flames on the roof, she punched him in the chest and knocked the wind out of him. "I told you to let me die!"

"Why," he hissed, "I was not trying to kill you."

"You want to kill Jai, so you're my enemy," she kicked fire at his face.

Zay was unfazed and rolled over, quickly dodging the flames, "Stop, you're just burning the roof faster! I'm not going to kill anyone. I wouldn't kill anyone without a good reason. I've done a lot of messed-up stuff, but I'm not a murderer. I hate Jai. Yes, I do. Sometimes the chance to kill him is freedom to me. But, I'd never be able to honor my mother's memory as a murderer," his eyes watered, then he chuckled, "I can't imagine tarnishing all of her . . . love like that." His eyes were glassy, almost as if he remembered a distant memory. Alena just watched him. He then shook his head. "If you want me to kill you, you'll have to give me a good reason; then I'll push you off this roof myself."

The fire danced around their feet as silence grew between them. They took minuscule steps toward each other, their gazes locked. Zay closed his eyes before looking down into the headquarters. In one fleeting moment, his dark brown eyes met her light brown ones, "Try and stay alive, okay? Good luck, Firefly," he stepped over and dropped down into the headquarters.

Alena was left alone on top of a flame-filled roof. Her heart was racing. There was an odd sensation threatening to consume her. She touched her heart as it battled against the rising tide of affection, each beat a defiant stand against the currents of attraction. Alena was in the crosshairs of a silent war between her desire to guard her heart and the magnetic force that sought to claim her.

CHAPTER 9

She peered over the edge where Zay had disappeared. "I should be his enemy, but he saved me," she murmured. She shook her head to free herself from the growing, conflicting emotions; she couldn't let him out of her sight. He said he wasn't a murderer but confessed to hating Jai. She just couldn't take a chance. At the last minute, Alena jumped over the edge and hurried to catch Zay. Jai was still her Legend, and she would not let any harm come to him.

She nimbly followed Zay, who led her straight to Agni and Jai. Agni appeared to have worn Jai down, his mask glistened from the flames that filled the room, and Jai looked tired.

"Now that I have you where I want you, I'll answer your question," Agni slowly walked toward Jai. Alena was about to walk into the room before a hand covered her mouth from behind her. She struggled against her opponent, but she was no match for his strength.

"I said try to stay alive. You can't go there if you don't want to die. If Agni could wear him down and I could wear you down, you wouldn't last long in there," Zay whispered, his breath tickling her ear.

Alena immediately stilled at hearing his voice. His breath on her ears ignited a fire making her face feel flushed.

"I am going to eradicate the Legends. They have brought the common people nothing but chaos and hell. And the brutal truth is, the Legends are not wanted anymore. Once upon a time, your kind was glorified. Then I started to ask why. Your kind has caused nothing but war, suffering, and Universal imbalance for the rest of us. And now, we're tired. We are tired of one person from each Nation being stronger than the rest of us. We are tired of being at your service. So, I proposed the idea of doing something that has never been done before," Agni stepped up to Jai, leaning on the wall and grabbing his right shoulder, which was bleeding profusely.

"There is a curse that I must break. However, to save the world from burning in eternal flames, you must die. You don't understand what is coming and what is truly at stake. You can't save the people, Jai. Your existence is the reason for the curse. So this is what I have to do. I'm going to break the cycle. I will save them from those destined to destroy it. Look, I've already shown the Firehearts that we can save ourselves and solve our own problems without a Legend. Don't worry. You're just the first one that I'm going to kill. Afterward, I'll hunt the rest of them before they are strong enough to take down an army. You just have the honor of dying first," the flames filled Agni's hand as he went to grab Jai's throat. Jai held it, burning it with light. Agni groaned as Jai kicked him in the core.

Zay let Alena go and ran into the room, "So you're just a murderer. You're using us to murder four people because they're stronger than you!" Zay eyed Jai and slightly motioned his head toward the opening. Jai looked at Zay, uncertain as to his intentions. Was it a trap? He thought about what Sheraga told him about not accepting mercy from his enemies. He stayed put, clutching his bloody shoulder.

Agni pushed Zay into a burning wall, and he hollered. Jai's eyes widened in shock that Agni would turn on his own soldier like that. Jai focused and manipulated the fire into a soft ball of light before hurling the ball like a violent beam at Agni. The beam cut the upper part of his arm. Zay groaned and turned over. Agni made a wall of fire around Jai, completely encasing him. He slowly walked through the firewall and held something close in his long sleeve.

Jai turned the firewall into a light wall, only for Agni to turn it back. The offensive wall flickered back and forth from fire to light to fire again.

"I'm impressed that you managed to learn this much control, Jai. It's a pleasant surprise that I have the honor of watching you fight to the death. I can't allow this curse to destroy anyone else. I will liberate the people. It doesn't matter who must meet their end. Future generations will thank me."

"No!" Alena ran inside and shot a burning arrow at Agni's head. He never turned toward her. Somehow he completely burned the arrow to ashes before it reached him. Jai punched fire with his right hand and kicked a light beam at Agni. He turned in a complete circle making a fire shield, defending himself from the attack. Zay pushed himself to his feet, trying to push Alena outside. He stopped and looked at his stomach. Agni stabbed right through him with his hand, covered in white lightning.

Zay's eyes fluttered, "Just run, Firefly," he fell to his knees before collapsing. Alena screamed at the top of her lungs as she watched Zay bleed. She hurried to his side and covered the gushing wound with her hands in a feeble attempt to stop the bleeding.

Agni sighed, "What a waste." He looked immune to the murder.

Jai felt his anger reaching a point of no return—Zay was trying to help him and Alena. Zay, murdered while standing to protect Alena. His eyes burned as Agni raised his hand toward Alena the moment Zay's body hit the floor with a gentle thud. He felt like his body was on fire.

Anger, a raging sensation, grew within, screaming for freedom. Jai yelled and a wild flame erupted from his mouth. As he charged Agni to the ground, he burned the mask onto his face. Agni yelled in pain. Alena was shooting her flaming arrows, but Agni could still burn them before they made contact. Then Jai felt a strange sensation creeping upon him. He couldn't move. His body became still so suddenly. He could only clearly hear the pounding of his heart.

"Jai," Alena called to him.

The room was filled with smoke and flames. Alena leaped over Zay and toward the last place she saw Jai. She dragged what she believed was his body toward the hall. Alena touched Jai, but he never moved. His eyes never opened. Agni was nowhere to be found. She hurried to pull Jai's body to safety. He was motionless. She then went back and looked at Zay's body. He wasn't dead yet, but he didn't have long. She also wanted to move him to safety but was afraid that any sudden movement would kill him instantly. She turned her back and ran back to Jai, hiding him as best as possible. Alena decided that she would stay with Jai and defend his motionless body until another Flamethrower found her. She peered at his face and sobbed. Alena felt like she had failed. And her failure cost two people their lives.

*****

Agni wiggled the mask around his face. He was only slightly burned. This did not bother him. He was slightly surprised by what had transpired. He didn't expect the Legend to have been that proficient. They normally aren't that powerful until they unite as four. He also didn't expect to be betrayed. However, he was not bothered. Zay would die soon, and the Legend would be dead by morning. The stupid girl could try whatever she wanted, but the die was already cast. He chuckled to himself. The only thing he cared about now was to salvage the rest of his soldiers.

He jumped to the first floor of his building, now decorated with flames, and began to assist the flames in burning everything down. The building started to crumble completely. The walls, once solid and steadfast, now quivered with an unsettling vulnerability. Dust danced in the air, particles set into chaotic motion by the building's convulsions. The deafening crackle of flames outside was matched only by the building's feeble protests against its inevitable fate. Each tremor served as a chilling reminder of the fiery turmoil consuming it.

Staggering in the swaying structure, Arrow watched Agni, "Everyone get out. It's gonna collapse." The

Flamethrowers fanned out desperately trying to escape. However, the stone building fell beneath them within seconds.

Calida's eyes watered as she saw the stone castle-like abode fall, and she could only think about her Flamethrowers. "No," she cried out, running toward the surrendering ruins.

"Calida, stop, don't go there," Cahya called out to his sister, but his words fell on deaf ears. Cahya, Yuuna, and Beamer continued to hold the soldiers back to the best of their ability.

"Ignite!" Calida screamed as she shot an arrow into the sky. A fiery phoenix flew down and scooped her up. She stood on the back of the fiery beast as Agni walked away from the ruins engulfed in flames. "Phoenix Rage," she screamed. A second phoenix erupted from the first and consumed Agni completely. His body was swallowed by the mouth of the phoenix. Just as suddenly, the second flaming beast retreated into the first one, "What?" Calida questioned.

Agni simply looked at the phoenix she stood on. The sky split and flashed white, and a massive lightning bolt erupted. Agni claimed control over the bolt and shot it with extreme precision through the phoenix Calida was riding, causing it to dissipate. Calida was over sixty feet in the air and plummeted ferociously into the burning building.

Cahya's heart dropped as his sister crashed into the ruins. "Calida!"

He fell back from fighting and screamed, "Ignite!"

His phoenix was twice the size of Calida's. The phoenix engulfed the last of Agni's soldiers. Yuuna and Beamer ran from the fiery wings of the massive phoenix to avoid being consumed along with the enemy. Agni's remaining soldiers took their last stand at that moment before burning to ashes from the rage of Cahya's loyal phoenix. Hate and bloodlust dominated Cahya's eyes as he shot violent spewing fire at Agni. His force was met with a hurling fire laced with lightning.

They seemed evenly matched before Agni started to saunter toward him, "Such raw power. You truly are a young master. I feel your strength pulsing through the flames," Agni marveled at Cahya's natural talent.

"Phoenix! Attack!"

Cahya's phoenix traveled through his spewing fire, creating a surge in Cahya's raw power. Yuuna and Beamer watched in disbelief at how powerful Cahya was; they had never seen him like this before. Smoke clouded the sky blackening out the sun.

With the additional strength of the phoenix, an explosion erupted. A massive bomb of fire, lightning, and smoke leveled everything within a one-mile radius. Cahya was flung backward into Yuuna and Beamer. The sheer impact of being slammed into the stone rubble of buildings rendered all three unconscious. Agni took a deep breath before reveling in the destruction of his surroundings. Only he was left standing.

That Pyrocean and Phoenix wielder truly had potential. What a shame to waste such young and talented young men. Hmm, even Arka's boy put up a good fight. What a shame to waste. But it had to be done.

Agni shook his head slightly. His soldiers had put up a relentless fight. That last phoenix wiped them out. However, all was not lost. Agni calmly walked away from the burning border as if nothing had happened.

CHAPTER 10

Boaz looked down and gulped. He was flying at a ridiculous speed, high in the air, getting smacked in the face continuously by lengthy waves of gunmetal-colored locks. He had left Kashmala about an hour ago and was almost to Kindle with the assistance of wild-haired Hova. She was very friendly and completely spontaneous. It took forever for her to make up her mind about which bird she was going to choose for the journey. She went back and forth between a needletail and a falcon. Saar kept insisting that she use the falcon. Still, she seemed more interested in comparing the speeds between the two so she could document it for research. At one point, she even suggested that they take both, each riding separately. Ultimately, thanks to Saar's insistence, she chose the falcon.

Boaz could not wait to get off the winged creature. Hova, on the other, seemed to be enjoying herself. She took her deep brown hands off the reins letting the wind flow between her fingers. "Don't kill me! I can't afford to die right now," Boaz groaned.

"Oh, I forgot you were scared," Hova replied, quickly grabbing the reins.

He frowned at her remarks, "I'm not scared, just uneasy about flying near the sun with someone who takes her hands off the reins," he grumbled.

"Yeah, yeah, just another way of saying scared," Hova giggled. She looked back with a purely mischievous twinkle in her slate-gray eyes. Reflecting, Boaz was glad he had gone to Kashmala. Kavi seemed to take the news about Aqila's disappearance seriously, and the Universe was definitely with him. He argued with the Wind Guardian, who happened to be Kavi's brother. And to top it off, Kavi was the mystery man Aqila's engaged to. Everything was working out in a very unusual way. He felt confident that if anyone could find Aqila, Kavi could.

"Are you doing okay back there?" Hova asked.

"Yeah, I guess," Boaz groaned.

"Hey, I don't know everything that's going on, but your friends are truly blessed to have you. You're determined to make sure things go right on their behalf. My favorite girl is going as fast as she can, and we should reach Kindle by nightfall, tops," Hova reassured.

"Thanks, I really appreciate it. Will you be staying?"

"Me? Of course not," she scoffed, "I plan on getting back ASAP to convince Saar to give me all the details about what's going on. I'm his best friend, and he has to fill me in." Hova was convinced that Saar would fill her in.

"Yeah, I hope that goes well," Boaz rolled his eyes.

"Wait, what's that supposed to mean?" Hova frowned at the thought of being left out.

"Nothing. So how long have you known Saar?" he decided to change the subject.

"My whole life. In Kashmala, we start going to school at four. Saar, Aqila, she's our apprentice seer, and I started school together. Our primary school is from ages four to seven. Secondary school is from seven to ten, and we prepare for specialty schools in whatever our interests are afterward. We started our first classes together. That first year was so fun. Saar and I sat beside each other during class. Aqila sat beside Kavi. They're both left-handed, so they always shared a desk. And that was the beginning for them," she giggled, "they really grew to like each other.

"That first day was so exhilarating! I remember it like it was yesterday. Aqila could have these mini visions about things that would happen the next day. That was always fun until things got out of hand. Students wanted her to have visions for them all the time, and she passed out with a bad nosebleed. Only Kavi could get them to back off and give her some space. Well, anyway, after our first year, Aqila skipped the second year and went to the third. Saar and I went to the second year. I can't remember ever having a class where we didn't share a desk . . . or when he didn't fall asleep and was scurrying to pass at the end of the year.

"After school," Hova continued, "the four of us would always spend time together trying new things or going to new places. It felt somewhat strange when Aqila went to secondary school without us, and I missed her in class, but we always made up for lost time after school. After secondary school, Saar started his apprenticeship with the WindGuard, and I went to school for Advanced Avian Biology. I would see Kavi at the Specialty School—he went for Advanced Chemistry and Advanced Mathematical Science."

"Did Aqila go to the Specialty School?" Boaz asked. He found Hova's childhood very interesting.

"She did for a year. She was in the science wing with Kavi and me. She completed the first level, Applied Astronomy, in one year. Awesome, right? The Applied level normally takes two years. Then her old mentor came for her, and she moved far away after that year to start her seer apprenticeship. She never got to finish the level two Associate or her level three Advanced Astronomy. That was a sad summer when her mentor came. And I disliked him for a long time for splitting us up. Then I learned that it was her destiny."

Hova signed, "When the Rulers Akash and Sufa announced to Kashmala and Wyndhm that Aqila was beginning her training as a seer, it felt like we were counting down to never seeing her again. Kavi and Saar begged their parents to allow Aqila time to visit, and they did. She could visit us one day a week. We were so happy! Aqila would save her time so we could have summer, birthdays, and holidays together. All in all, we were always okay."

"Hold up. Kavi and Saar's parents are the Rulers of Kashmala?" Boaz's jaw dropped.

"Yes," Hova replied, unimpressed.

"So, I was arguing with the son of a ruler? Great," he mumbled.

"What was that?"

"Um, what made you want to enter Advanced Avian Science?"

"Advanced Avian Biology," she corrected, "I love birds! Always have, always will! They are so amazing. And I love researching the species bred for riding, and it's interesting. Birds actually do a lot for Wyndhm and Kashmala's natural ecosystem."

Hova patted the neck of the falcon, and it began to do tight spirals upward. Boaz's teeth were chattering as he dug his fingers into Hova's arms.

"Why are you squeezing me?"

"Please, stop!"

"Oh yeah, sorry! I got excited! Dive!"

"Holy Stars!"

Hova's hands released the reins as the falcon dove at top speed. If her hair wasn't covering his face, Boaz would have thrown up all of his internal organs. The rush of wind and hair nearly suffocated him. Then a calm passed over him as they returned to flying at a steady pace.

"I keep forgetting! Sorry, I didn't mean to scare you."

He sighed. He disliked being called scared, but he decided to own it on this occasion.

"Okay, I promise I'll focus, and I won't get carried away. Can't have you passing out, throwing up, or having a heart attack— then you won't be able to do what you gotta do . . . whatever that is. Either way, Saar will tell me." Hova giggled.

Boaz found it hard not to smile at Hova's antics. It seemed like growing up as a Windmaster was nice. He couldn't imagine what it must have been like growing up free from a civil war. He looked to the sky. It was getting late, and dusk was coming onto the horizon. He hoped that Aqila was all right. He had to find Sheraga and give him the message. He just prayed that he wasn't too late. He closed his eyes and sighed.

Moss-eyed Ila appeared before him, eroding the darkness behind his eyelids, "Concentrate on doing your best, and you won't have to worry about being too late," she spoke in a gentle whisper.

It's almost nightfall. What if I took too long to get help? What if something happened to Aqila already? What if something happened to Jai? He's the Legend. I don't want to live with their deaths forever in my conscience.

Ila disappeared, and a man rose in her place. He was broad-shouldered with cool, brown skin. His eyes were a deep shade of blue, and his wild waves of silky black hair fell just past his shoulders, "Does anything happen without the Universe knowing? Do you believe that they control these stars?"

Nothing happens without the Universe.

The blue-eyed man disappeared, and Basir arose, "What Aenon was telling you is to keep your faith. Everything happens for a reason. If someone is meant to live, the Universe ensures that they live. However, the Universe ensures they pass if someone's time has come. As you do not fear life, you should not fear death. We all live because someone died." Basir slowly faded away.

Boaz opened his eyes. Ila, Aenon, and Basir's presence refueled his confidence. Although some things Basir said went over his head.

An hour of silence passed. He was slowly getting more comfortable in the plush seat of the riding mat.

It reminded him of his dear Aqila, who preferred riding bareback. Now that he was experiencing the sky for the second time, he was clueless as to how she did that. Hova kept her promise; she was laser-focused on navigating through the skies. Boaz was a little surprised that the slender giant actually could focus.

"We're in Kindle now. Do you know where Sheraga is staying?" Hova asked, thoroughly shaking Boaz from his thoughts.

"Um, well, he's staying with Tora," Boaz replied.

"Hm, is that so? All right, my favorite girl will have you there in half an hour, won't you, Swift," she cooed to the falcon. The bird squawked in response, maintaining its speed.

Boaz was concerned about finding Sheraga. He wasn't sure how he would explain everything that Aqila told him. Would Sheraga believe him? He has a reputation for being hot-headed and battle-ready. He had never met a Pyrocean. He had only heard rumors that they were half-human and half-dragon, with near-godlike abilities with fire. And Sheraga was not just any Pyrocean but the DragonLord with a dangerous reputation.

The DragonLord's family took being a Fireheart to an entirely different level. Some of them, like Sheraga, were able to physically transform into a dragon. Growing up through a civil war taught Boaz that people like that can be complicated to reason with. He only hoped that Sheraga was not too difficult. Also, he was concerned about being in Kindle. Theyra and Kindle had strained relationships, and the last thing he wanted to do was trigger another war. He didn't want an incident like what happened on the Kashmalan border— even though Saar didn't really help in that situation. Determined to do his best for Aqila's sake, he decided to be more cautious in dealing with the Firehearts than he had been with the Windmasters. Generally, they were more peaceful-natured people. However, Boaz knew he needed to learn from his mistakes.

The smell of sand filled Boaz's nostrils as they continued through Kindle's sky. Dusk was approaching swiftly, and Boaz needed time to find Sheraga, Tora, or both.

"Thanks for bringing me here. You made good time," Boaz thanked Hova.

"Anytime. I hope your journey continues to progress." As she landed Swift, Boaz jumped off the falcon's back and grabbed his things. He gently stroked Swift's brown, feathery face, "Thank you," he whispered. He headed to his left.

"Landkeeper, wait!"

Boaz turned as Hova called him, "Yes?"

"Tora's place is the other way. Look for a sandstone house with textured glass double front doors. I think he has hot stones for a door mat too. You can't miss it," she explained as Swift hovered off the ground.

"Thanks, Hova." Boaz waved. She nodded, and Swift flew off, back in the direction of Kashmala. Even at top speed, she wouldn't be back home until tomorrow if she didn't stop for the night. The desert of Kindle was different from the Theyran Desert. Back home, there were a few oases that sparked life in mini towns, like the one he lived in. However, this desert was highly populated. He did not see any houses yet, but when he focused, he could feel structures up ahead through the soles of his feet.

Boaz walked through the desert regarding the location of the structures he was sure were houses. After another half hour had passed, a village came into view. It was getting darker, so he began to run to the village. He ran past a few dunes, and there he was, looking over the village. However, despair began to creep into his heart. Hova made it seem like Tora's place would be obvious to find. However, most homes here were sandstone, and he could see several glass front doors.

"Ugh, and she said I wouldn't miss it," Boaz groaned. He took a deep breath and continued forward. He had to find Sheraga before it got too dark. As he traveled through the city, the smell of fire filled his nostrils, and the presence of smoke burned his eyes.

"How do they live here?" he murmured to himself.

Boaz began feeling frustrated—he found several sandstone homes, glass doors, and hot stone door mats. He wished Hova had taken him straight to Tora's place. Well, she couldn't do that with Swift. But it would have been helpful if she had come with him. Well, it wasn't like she knew exactly what was going on to understand how imperative it was that he found Sheraga. All she knew was that she needed to get him to Kindle.

After a mile of walking, Boaz looked to see the sun almost completely gone for the day. He sighed.

If anyone wants to come out and point me in the direction of the right house, be my guest.

No one answered. Boaz became frustrated by the lack of response and began thrashing at the air as he walked. This earned him nervous glances from the citizens of Kindle. Boaz stopped, not wanting to draw too much attention to himself. He heard a feminine giggle but saw no one. He listened to the laughter again.

"The young Windmaster told you what you needed to know. Details, Bo, details. Look for a sandstone house with textured glass double front doors." The voice reminded him.

"Oh yeah, textured glass double doors, thanks, Cyra." Boaz continued for another ten minutes, hastily searching for the house. Panic was beginning to set in as he thought about the approaching darkness. He was still in enemy territory. He truly felt lost wandering around the unfamiliar desert city.

The Universe was with him, for as the darkness filled the sky, he found a sandstone house with textured glass double doors. He ran toward the door, carefully avoiding the hot stone doormat, and feverishly knocked on the door.

He's the leader of Kindle, maybe I should not have knocked like that.

"Who is it?" a man's voice yelled out, irritation in his tone.

"It's an emergency. I need Tora or Sheraga," Boaz replied. He waited for several minutes without an answer. Suddenly the door opened. A tall young man with warm, brown skin opened the door. His eyes were an intense hazel, "You're looking for me?"

"You're Tora?" Boaz questioned as he was allowed to step inside. He looked around the sandstone house. It was pretty nice but not extravagant. The walls were a light beige, and there were firelit lamps in every corner. On one wall was a long clawfoot sofa with red embroidered cushions. Stretched out on this sofa was an extravagantly dressed Pyrocean with long, blood-red hair. Boaz exclaimed, "You're Sheraga! I have a message for you from Aqila."

Tora and Sheraga looked at each other with questioning looks. Tora burst into laughter, "What would a seer want with the likes of you? Look, we both are acquaintances of hers. If she had a message, she'd send it herself," Tora hissed, lightning encasing his fingers,

"So come again, what do you want?" He raised his lightning-covered pointer finger to Boaz's forehead. Sadly, Boaz understood Tora's disdain for him. Theyra has been leeching off Kindle's already small territory. Lightning would prove deadly to him if Tora actually released it. His sage eyes glared into Tora's hazel ones. The aggressive energy was palpable.

Sheraga laughed, "Tora, as a leader, I would not expect you to be so rough with your guest. Let him continue telling us his elaborate and thrilling story."

Boaz was irritated. Seeing that Tora appeared to be nearly the same age as himself, he wanted to give him a piece of his mind. He contemplated using his ability to send the leader of Kindle's house crumbling down, but he sighed and thought about Aqila. She trusted him.

"Aqila came to my parent's library this morning to return her books. She told me that she needed to have a death vision and thought it had something to do with Jai, the Legend. She told me of her journey to Pyroc and meeting the Legend. She also mentioned the message she passed to you, Sheraga, about Agni. She expressed her concerns about Agni's intentions. Aqila went outside to have her vision—then she went missing."

Sheraga sat up straight, "What do you mean missing?"

"She has had visions before, and she'd go out past the dunes near the border. Talon was outside going amuck, which made me look for her. I waited for her, but she was nowhere to be found. I went to Kashmala, argued with the guard, met Aqila's fiancé, and flew on a falcon's back with a crazy lady just to get here. The bottom line is that Aqila had a vision about Jai being in danger."

"Come on, Sheraga, you're not buying this, really? A Landkeeper and a Windmaster, friends? A Legend needs saving? Legends, who are more powerful than us, come on. Give me a break," Tora groaned.

Sheraga spoke slowly, "He's not lying, Tora. It's all the truth." He stood up. Tora's eyes went wide with disbelief.

"You met the Legend and never said anything," Tora gasped.

"Do you know who I am? I don't have to explain my business to you. I have to go, my brother was with Jai. If they are in danger, I need to help them," Sheraga started for the door.

"Sheraga wait! Aqila's still an apprentice seer. Are you sure this isn't a mistake? You can't afford to damage your reputation. You're the DragonLord. I'll go in your stead," Tora offered.

"No, I need you here. Tora, you're the leader and a young one at that. Your enemies will take advantage of your absence. As for Aqila, the last time she told me of a death vision, she was deadly accurate. Depending on what's going on, I may need to bring someone back here," Sheraga explained.

"Of course, in circumstances like this, my house is yours."

"What's your name, Landkeeper?" Sheraga asked.

"Boaz of Theyra."

"Well, Boaz, come with me. Then you can accurately report back to Kashmala." Sheraga walked past Boaz and continued outside.

"What about Aqila? Is anyone looking for her?" Tora asked.

"Kavi was going to look for her," Boaz answered.

"If anyone can find her, it's him. Sorry I brushed you off earlier," Tora shook Boaz's hand, "Sheraga's preparing to leave. You've come a long way so take Magma." Tora escorted Boaz outside and around to the back of the sandstone house. A giant Gila monster was saddled and ready for riding. Tora looked at Boaz. "Can you ride her?"

"I'd rather ride this than the bird again. Will she allow me to ride her?"

"Yeah," he motioned for Boaz to follow him. He strapped a clear cubed lantern around the Gila monster's neck and shot lightning in the lantern until it ignited a flame. Afterward, he sealed the lantern. "Since you're not a Fireheart, she'll let you ride with this. She's a reptile, so she loves feeling the heat this close to her scales. This neck light will suffice. She's pretty easy to handle. Now, if she bites, it is poisonous, but as long as you're not stupid, you'll be fine."

Boaz easily mounted Magma and pulled the reins to get her to move. Like Tora said, she was straightforward to handle. Sheraga rode his Komodo dragon around the back and asked, "Boaz, you coming?"

"Yeah, I'm coming." Magma quickly followed Sheraga's reptile, Boaz turned to Tora, "Thanks."

Tora nodded them off. As the night grew, the pair headed toward Ember. Boaz was thankful that Sheraga believed him and prayed that the Legend would be all right until they arrived.

CHAPTER II

It was night in the Snow Tribe. Tiber had returned with Mika, and they slept peacefully, huddled far away from Aqila. As tired as she was, Aqila didn't trust her body to sleep. She needed to stay awake to consciously oxygenate her body. She didn't want to fall asleep and never wake up again. Her body had regained feeling to her knees. At this rate, she would have sensation in her entire body again by morning. Aqila was devising a plan of escape. If she could make it just to Wyndhm, one of the apothecary shops would have something that would hold her until she got back to Kashmala for an antidote. While Tiber was sleeping with her back semi-turned, Aqila quickly loosened the ropes around her ankles. She decided she would make her escape by morning.

Aqila felt a familiar sensation behind her eyes. A vision was brewing. Images briefly began to flash before her eyes. Her heart sank. Every image was so filled with blood that she could not make anything out. Not a person, not a place, not a thing. She sighed. Suddenly, footsteps approached. Aqila quickly closed her eyes.

"Ugh, this girl is sleeping on the job." It was Nahal's voice. Aqila slowed her breathing down to imitate sleep. "Good thing the Windmaster is immobile, or that would have been a problem." Aqila heard his footsteps come closer. His cold hands checked her neck for a pulse. "You're a strong one, aren't you?" he whispered.

She heard his steps grow distant before stopping. He seemed to have sat down. Unfortunately for Aqila, staying awake with her eyes closed like this was proving impossible. Sleep threatened to claim her. She stifled a yawn. She didn't want to give Nahal any reason to believe she was awake.

Aqila knew that she wouldn't be able to keep up like this.

I'm going to end up falling asleep at this rate. Maybe if I stay up long enough to regain feeling throughout my body, sleep won't be harmful to my escape.

She slowly fluttered her eyes open. Nahal was sitting near Tiber. However, he wasn't looking in her direction. This made Aqila feel slightly relieved. She closed her eyes and focused on oxygenating the rest of her body. She felt the pressure behind her eyes increase. Images flickered in her mind once again. Fiery wings, red scales, and blood flashed into her view. She saw flashes of red hair and then a blinding light. A light so bright that it seemed to burn through her eyelids.

What could that mean?

Aqila was puzzled. She was almost sure that the light referred to Jai, and if so, the red hair had to be either Arrow or Sheraga. The red scales seemed to refer to either Sheraga or Bhasker—or possibly both of them. The fiery wings were a mystery to her. However, the blood scared fear. Blood could mean pain, injury, or, at worst, death. Aqila was frustrated. She couldn't even sit up straight and align her body to properly receive the vision. Flashes came again. The fiery wings flapped, then they faded and transformed into bird wings. The plumage looked like a Great Gray.

The pattern almost looked like Talon's wings. Did Talon know where she was? Was he coming to help her? Was it Talon or possibly Sterling? Was Kavi on the way? Aqila pressed the images for answers prematurely. In doing so, she lost the image completely. She sighed heavily.

That was a mistake, she knew better than that. Her forceful exhale captured the attention of Nahal. She heard him stand up and walk over toward her. Aqila calmed herself. She felt his breath tickle her face. She breathed slowly and deliberately. Nahal didn't move for several minutes. Aqila was unsure how long she could suppress the sensation behind her eyes. The last thing she wanted was for Nahal to suspect that she possibly had a vision. Finally, he moved away from her. His footsteps went closer to where Tiber was sleeping.

That was close. I can't be so careless.

Aqila tried to focus on the vision, grateful that she was still able to have one. The Universe was giving her a sign of hope to hold onto. She'd always held onto a sliver of hope that she would make it through this, but after receiving a vision, there was no doubt that she would make it. She heard stirring near where the Waterbearers were.

"Nahal!" Tiber sounded surprised.

"Who else would it be?" he replied sarcastically.

Tiber yawned and stretched her legs, careful to not kick Mika. "Did you hear anything? Do you have the antidote?"

"No, I came to see how things were going with the Windmaster. She's not dead yet," Nahal replied.

"She's been slow the entire evening. She may die by morning," Tiber whispered sorrowfully.

"Nah, she'll be fine. I checked her pulse when I came in, and it was slow but strong. Somehow, she's adjusting to the poison. Her body is still stiff, so I think she's still paralyzed. If things keep going at this rate, you may have a chance."

"A chance for what?"

"If she's still alive, you have more time to get answers from her. Besides, if her body is adjusting, she may be able to have a vision. That's all we need," Nahal replied.

"Yeah, but how will we know if she's lying to us?" Tiber asked.

"Don't be a child, Tiber. Let's say she has a vision. We'll take her with us when we look for the Legend. If there's no sign that he was where she told us he'd be, she's lying. If she lies, we'll send her straight to Neptune to do with her as he pleases."

"Well, I guess that's a plan, but you're banking so hard on her having a vision. If she can't move, why are you so sure she'll have one?"

"I'm not sure. I just have a feeling. Anyway, you can't be sleeping while you have a hostage."

"Chill, will you! Like you said, she can't move. There's nothing to worry about," Tiber brushed off Nahal's concern.

"Okay, if Neptune catches you sleeping on a mission, you'll be missing a head. Keep letting your guard down. See where it gets you," Nahal growled.

"Why do you have to be so serious about every little thing? Maybe if you came back earlier, we could have alternated watching her," Tiber spat. "We need to keep it down so we don't wake her."

"I don't care. If she wakes up, we can question her," Nahal shrugged.

"I questioned her all day. She didn't get to the part of the vision that told her where the Legend is," Tiber reminded Nahal.

"Yeah, because you went crazy and decided to pour a whole syringe full of the drug into her neck." Tiber sighed and looked down at her hands. Nahal bumped his shoulder into hers, "It'll be okay. Don't stress about it too much."

"Yeah, says the man who stresses about everything," Tiber rolled her eyes. "I just didn't realize how bad I would feel if her health turns for the worst and she dies. If she dies, it would be my fault. Everything I'm doing is to keep people from dying, but I don't want to kill a person to achieve that."

"There's nothing else to do. Neptune has the antidote. We can't get to him now, and you can't take back what has already happened. It is what it is," Nahal replied, nonchalantly.

"How is Neptune so powerful?"

"Don't know, don't care. Why do you ask?"

"I don't know. It just came to mind. I was thinking about how he would save our people in exchange for these favors we do for him and got curious about his power," Tiber explained.

"Like I said, I don't know, and I don't care. Neptune should be worshiped. Our tribe is so much better because of him. We have a new avenue of resources and are starting to see some growth and advancement. Neptune will protect us with his power and influence. If anyone can save us, he can."

"If this goes south anymore, I won't get the chance to see any of that," Tiber groaned.

"Then you have to do everything you can to keep things from going south. You have to be willing to do whatever it takes." Nahal shrugged before yawning, "I'm going to sleep." He turned and curled into a ball.

"You know, alternating sleep was my idea."

Nahal turned around, "And?" He turned his back to Tiber, trying to go to sleep.

"Whatever," she muttered.

Aqila knew things would get more complicated if she didn't escape tomorrow. She knew that Tiber was awake because she could hear her moving around. Aqila reflected on Tiber. She had not been claimed by the moon yet; because of that, her body frame was still childlike. She could turn ice into water, but she did not see anything extraordinary about her ability. Also, since she did not believe in the Universe, she probably was not gifted enough to be too powerful.

It would not be wise to try to escape or attack at night. Waterbearers are at their peak strength in the presence of the moon and stars. Aqila had never seen Tiber at her peak. Nahal was a different story. His mindset was cold and calculating. Aqila knew that abilities and personality types were closely linked. This could make Nahal dangerous. Regardless, with her body not at total capacity, she was unwilling to have an altercation with Tiber and Nahal at night. She would have to slip out first thing in the morning. Tiber would be tired and Nahal would be slightly disoriented, having just awakened. Aqila planned on using this to her advantage.

Aqila did not know how many of the Snow Tribe supported Neptune. That could be problematic. If the entire tribe was on Neptune's side, she would have to fight tooth and nail to escape. She had to escape in the early morning. Aqila fluttered her eyes open for a moment. She saw Tiber standing at the ice cave entrance, looking out at the sky. She wondered why Tiber didn't tell Nahal about their conversations. They seemed to have an unusual relationship. However, Aqila could tell that if it came down to it, Nahal would sacrifice Tiber to save himself. Tiber was foolish enough not to recognize that already.

Unfortunately, Aqila also believed that Tiber was foolish enough to think that Nahal was entirely on her side.

As she continued to oxygenate her body, Aqila wondered if she would be ready to kill Tiber. Tiber was a young adult who tasted many misfortunes already and was primarily a victim of circumstance. She doesn't believe in the Universe because no one taught her the power of believing. Could she kill her if it came down to it? Aqila did not feel comfortable with the idea of killing Tiber. Although to save her life she may have to fight the Snow Tribe to the death, something didn't feel right about taking Tiber's life. Killing in the absence of war was not the way of the Windmasters and was completely against their values. But was this war? In a way, it was, as kidnapping her was equal to kidnapping a ruler. This was a war of sorts . . .

Aqila again felt pressure behind her eyes. It was not as intense as before. Images quickly came into her gifted mind's eye. A circle—divided into four equal parts. The upper left quarter of the circle had Jai's eyes. The light in his eyes was so intense yet oddly gentle. It was as if he was right in front of her. The upper right quarter showed Windmasters in a line. When Aqila focused on the details of the Windmasters, their faces had no features until the last one. She was shocked to see the face of the last Windmaster. It was Zeroun. A knot formed in Aqila's stomach. She had been so consumed by a recent vision that she'd left her home in the mountains without notice to anyone. Not her mentor, fiancé, or friends knew that she had left. Seeing Zeroun's face so vividly in the vision weighed her heart down with guilt.

The lower right quarter revealed nothing but a midnight sky with a bright, ivory full moon glowing against a dark velvety sky. The last quarter showed sand and lava. This fourth piece of the circle played with her senses. She heard a voice; she knew the sound, but she could not determine what the voice was saying. Then there was the smell of paper and ink. Something about it felt oddly comforting to Aqila. The images stopped. She was puzzled and confused.

What's going on with me? I have never had two separate visions on the same day. With two completely different messages. What could this mean?

Aqila pondered over the images. Could it be about the identity of the Legends? She wasn't sure. It was not unusual for seers to have Legend visions. The last one to experience this was Zeroun's mentor, Master Veda. However, in the second quarter, the only one with a face was Zeroun. He couldn't be a Legend. He's three hundred years old. The Fireheart is always first, so maybe it's someone Zeroun knows. But again, he's three hundred years old. He has to know a lot of people. Also, it might not be referring to the Legends at all. Aqila decided to let it go. She didn't have enough images that she understood to interpret the vision. Besides, her priority was set, escaping with as little bloodshed as possible. Sitting still and feigning sleep, she realized she had sensations throughout her entire body. Aqila wiggled her toes in her shoes to ensure this moment was real. She was thrilled, and utterly exhausted, but thrilled nonetheless.

Freedom had only been a mere whisper before, but it was calling for her now. She felt confident that she would return to her usual self. Aqila clung to patience with all her might. She didn't want to blow her chance. She smiled slightly as she allowed sleep to slowly take her into its folds, knowing she needed the rest to execute her plans. A part of her wondered how she managed this. Nahal and Tiber were so sure that she was going to stay paralyzed. They were so confident that she would be dead by morning.

However, that did not seem to be the case. Maybe because she's a Storm, and her captors were unaware of that was the edge she needed to beat this. She wasn't entirely sure.

Aqila silently prayed that Jai and the Flamethrowers were all right. The visions of blood greatly disturbed her. Never in her life had she had a vision like that. Not even her death visions were that gory. This truly concerned Aqila. Then there was the puzzle of the mystery vision with a meaning she could not comprehend.

When I return to Kashmala, I'll share that vision with Zeroun. He might know what it means.

Based on the angles she knew how to analyze, it did not add up. Thinking like this was tiring, especially after the day's ordeals. After resisting sleep as long as she could, Aqila could hold out no longer and finally drifted off.

CHAPTER 12

Aqila awoke. Her vision was slightly hazy from sleep. Just as she expected, Tiber had fallen asleep near the ice cave entrance. Nahal and Mika were still fast asleep, having never moved from last night. Aqila's hands had been free since earlier yesterday. Her body felt awkward with every movement.

Whatever that drug was has left me somewhat stiff.

With extreme caution, she crawled to the cave entrance, completely silent. Aqila felt an intense tearing sensation in the muscles in her arms and legs. The searing pain felt like her body was being ripped apart from the inside out. Each movement was agony, and every breath she took was a struggle. The pain shot down her arms and legs like lightning. After all she had already endured, Aqila felt as though her body was betraying her. Every movement felt like its own battle. Even the slightest twitch sent relentless waves of excruciating pain through her body. It took all of her discipline not to cry out. She gritted her teeth, took a deep breath, and forced herself to move forward, no matter how much it hurt. She could hear the gentle sounds of Tiber's breathing as she fought to crawl past her.

Taking more effort than she expected, Aqila's hands and knees came into contact with the snow. The cold, fluffy snow completely covered the ground, and when she looked up, all she could see was a white blur. Escaping would be more complicated than Aqila had imagined, but she was determined to give her best effort. The pain was pulsing through her body, making her feel weak. Why now, of all times? She scolded herself. Suddenly, she felt the wind being knocked out of her. Aqila collapsed into the snow face-first and groaned in pain and exhaustion. She turned over, meeting those cold blue eyes of Nahal.

He grabbed her by the throat, "Where did you think you were going, huh?"

Aqila mustered the strength to lock his wrist, forcing him to let her go. She coughed as she inhaled heavily after dropping into the snow. She kicked Nahal in the shin. He kicked her in the rib cage, causing Aqila to scream in pain. Nahal began to drag her back to the cave. Aqila tried to do a wind kick. Her foot connected with his abdomen, but no wind followed. Fear drove its way into Aqila's heart as she realized she could not harness the power of her element.

"Nahal, what are you doing?" Tiber stormed out of the cave and tried to pull him away from Aqila.

With one shove Nahal pushed Tiber backward into the cave, her back slamming into the icy wall. She groaned in pain. "Traitor, you untied her!" Nahal struggled with Aqila. Her sheer height and intense leg power were proving difficult for Nahal to handle, even without her wind abilities. Tired of fighting with the Windmaster, who had kicked his shins until they were bleeding, he doused her with water until she could barely breathe. Water quickly flowed from his fingers to cocoon Aqila in multiple sheets of ice. Once frozen, he left her outside. Pure fury gleamed in his eyes as he violently marched toward Tiber.

"Nahal, stop! I didn't untie her, and I don't know how that happened. Are you sure you tied a knot?" Tiber questioned. Her heart was racing, and she was trembling, afraid of Nahal's evident anger.

"What do you think? Of course, I tied it! Maybe that's why you couldn't get any information. You were going to free her, and I can't believe I fell for your lies." His cerulean eyes were hungry with hatred.

"I did not free her, honestly, I didn't. Stop being so paranoid. We're on the same side, remember? I'm staying with Neptune until my sister's life is safe, and I mean it. Now back off." Tiber pushed Nahal away.

"I don't trust you—" Nahal growled.

"Nahal, lo—" Tiber started.

"Don't cut me off! I don't trust how you've been handling her. Then you fall asleep on your watch, not once but twice. When I woke up, you were asleep again, after you told me we would alternate," he yelled.

"Yes, I tried to wake you up after a few hours, but you didn't! So, I tried to stay awake, but I had a three-hour journey, and you didn't. Besides—" she stopped.

"Besides, what?"

"She's getting away!" Tiber pointed.

Nahal rolled his eyes, "That's crap. I froze her." He slowly turned, following Tiber's finger. To his disbelief, the Windmaster was hobbling away, free from most of the ice.

"Nahal, don't! One wrong move, and she'll fall over the edge to her death," Tiber pulled at his arm.

Nahal snatched himself away, "At this point, if she dies, it doesn't matter. Once again, it's your fault." He sent a wave of water toward Aqila. She looked back, stopped between the edge of the mountain and a wave of water. Aqila decided to press her luck with the mountain. Pain radiated throughout her entire body. As the wave threatened to consume her, she threw herself over the edge.

The wind was rushing past her at such a speed that breathing was difficult. The cold air sent sharp pangs through her lungs. This would not bother her if she were in control of her wind ability. Aqila focused on trying to make the best of her landing as she watched the icy river beneath her get closer and closer. She inhaled to brace herself for the cold water. Instead, her body firmly landed on a warm feathery body. Aqila rolled on her back, gasping for air, "Talon!"

The Great Gray squawked in reply. Her body was stiffening. All of her progress was rapidly going backward. Aqila turned and struggled to grab the reins of her dasher.

Talon screeched and began to dive downward. Aqila looked up. Nahal and Tiber were looking over the edge of the mountain. Her hands felt oddly warm and wet, blood. Talon was bleeding. He crashed near the river, and the impact knocked Aqila off his back. She tumbled through the snow desperately trying to catch her breath.

Aqila heard the sound of footsteps running toward her and Talon. Nahal and Tiber had expertly manipulated the snow on the mountain to effortlessly slide down the side. Aqila struggled to her feet; her head was pounding, and her body was so weak she could barely stand. Tiber stood near the icy river in a fighting stance.

Nahal smirked, "I'm really impressed. The average person would have been dead by now. I don't know how you did it, but your little venture ends here. Neptune's reinforcements are minutes away. You can't escape, Windmaster. Sorry, I had to kill your dumb bird, but Neptune's wishes must be fulfilled. This is your last chance to tell me where the Legend is, Windmaster! Tell us and you'll live!"

Aqila took a deep breath. The sensation of the oxygen filled her entire body and brought a calming clarity to her mind, "Aqila, my name is Aqila."

Nahal narrowed his eyes, "Wrong answer."

As the footsteps closed in on her, water ran from Nahal and Tiber's fingers and shot violently toward her. Aqila blocked the water with her windblade, allowing a furious wind gust to meet the icy water. Although she was not at her full prowess, she had what she needed. Oxygen manipulation! She opened her hands, palms up toward the river, and the water dissipated quickly. Nahal and Tiber looked in shock as the river seemed to be disappearing right before their eyes.

While they were in awe, Neptune's reinforcements arrived. Snow tribe men rushing on foot to surround her. Aqila blasted them back with a powerful wind blast knocking most of them unconscious. Something whizzed passed Aqila's head and shot Nahal straight in the chest. He groaned in pain.

"Nahal!" Tiber ran to him. Aqila looked around. She was sure that the tiny dart protruding from Nahal's chest was meant for her. Some of the reinforcements were regaining consciousness. Tiber charged at Aqila with all of her strength. She used the last water droplets left from the icy river to attack. She was resourceful, able to make only a few drops of water multiply.

"You're trying to kill us!" Tiber exploded, sending an ice shard toward Aqila's face.

Aqila deflected the shard and blasted Tiber several feet backward with a wind gust. She inhaled and exhaled, finding harmony in her breathing. Despite the pain she felt physically, Aqila's mind was quite alert. "I'm not trying to kill anyone. I'm leaving." Aqila used a wind kick, knocking Tiber onto the snow-covered ground as soon as she tried to stand back up. Turning her attention to the reinforcements, she noticed that they were slashed, some to the neck, others to the abdomen. She had not heard anything.

I have to be careful.

Tiber turned the snow into running water underneath her and Aqila, creating waves, ice shards, and ice sheets near Aqila's feet. She armed herself, turning water into ice daggers, and charged at Aqila. Despite being surrounded by water and ice, Aqila flipped Tiber and kicked her in the back, making her drop the dagger. The clouds in the sky instantly became dark and stormy. Aqila felt a surge of power like nothing she had ever experienced. Thunder was deafening to all ears but her own. With her right hand, she snatched Tiber backward by her hair, the Waterbearer groaning in pain. With her left hand, she gently covered Tiber's mouth and nose.

Tiber's eyes went wide. She couldn't breathe—unable to inhale or exhale. She fought to bring her hands up to pull Aqila's hand away, but her wind technique was unfazed by Tiber's struggle. The rest of her body started to tremble from suffocation. How did she become so powerful? A mighty wind was tunneling from the left and right. The tornadoes were scattering the bodies of Neptune's reinforcements like a war had taken place. The Windmaster was powerful enough to summon a storm while suffocating someone. Tiber realized that Aqila wasn't just any Windmaster but a powerful Storm.

CHAPTER 13

Her dark blue eyes met Aqila's silver ones for the first time; they locked onto each other's gaze. Aqila's eyes were angry yet beautiful and glistening Her orbs were a glorious twinkling shade of silver. Tiber felt her struggles come to an end as her eyes watered.

Aqila surprised herself at being able to storm while being so physically weak. Tiber's eyes locked onto hers. Aqila hated the feeling. The Waterbearer's eyes were glossy, pleading for life. Aqila manipulated the oxygen around her airways, leaving Tiber unable to breathe in or out. She was suffocating.

Suddenly, she recalled her vision! The circle from her flickered into her mind's eye, the image of the moon wouldn't escape her mind. The moon was pulsating between a bright glow and darkness. The longer she suffocated, the darker the image became. Although fury filled her blood, Aqila knew better than to play with a sign from the Universe. She didn't understand the vision but knew she couldn't kill Tiber.

I-I can't do it.

Going against everything she felt inside and holding onto her belief in the Universe, as Tiber's dark blue eyes were about to close for the last time, Aqila moved her hand. Tiber fell face-first into the snow.

Aqila turned to see the familiar dark gray harem pants and long blue tunic hovering over Nahal's body. She beamed with happiness.

"To be poisoned to death, you sure put up one hell of a fight," Kavi turned to face her. Aqila staggered, collapsing into his arms. Kavi caught her, "I'm here now. It's going to be okay. I have to give you this." He pulled a vial with a golden liquid from his pants pocket. He whistled for his dasher, Sterling. Moments later, she dove and landed right beside him.

Kavi lifted Aqila so she could sit on Sterling's back, "Open your mouth and stick out your tongue," Kavi gently tilted Aqila's head to get a good view inside her mouth, "Your tongue and the inside of your mouth are blue. Drink half of this." He gave her the vial.

Aqila drank half and sighed, "That feels better already."

"It's the antidote. I'll explain later," Kavi murmured. Aqila returned the vial to him with half of the antidote left.

Antidote?

"What are we going to do?" she asked hesitantly.

"He is poisoned," pointing to Nahal, "it should run its complete course in a few days, maybe a week. As for them," pointing to the reinforcements, "I covered my sword in a paralyzing poison. Most of them will die. Only you know when the girl should be coming back around."

"I don't know. I got a vision leading me to believe that I should not kill her," Aqila sighed. She was disturbed at how nonchalant Kavi seemed about killing the men of the Snow Tribe.

"Well, we don't argue with our gifts. Talon should be fine; it looks like he has a surface wound. We will hover through the mountain pass and drop him off at the bird sanctuary in Wyndhm to have him checked out. We should get going before the Snow Tribe arrives." Kavi mounted

Sterling in front of Aqila. She held onto his tunic carefully as they lifted into the air. As they rose, she called Talon, and he slowly followed Sterling's lead. As they flew higher into the air, Avala became a blur of white as the Great Gray owls flew away together back toward their home in Kashmala.

"Thank you for coming to get me, Kavi. I'm so sorry I put you in a position to have to kill like that. I know that is not our way," she murmured into his back.

"Don't apologize, they got what they deserved."

"That could ruin your reputation! Everything you worked for-"

"Means nothing if I lose you! Aqila, I love you. My reputation will never come before your safety. I would have killed a thousand times for a thousand lifetimes to protect you."

"Kavi-"

"Aqila," Kavi rested one hand on her knee, "you complete me. What kind of man would I be if I didn't risk it all for the one I love?"

Silence enveloped them as her eyes were on the brink of tears.

"I'm glad you received the wind song."

"A testament of true love. We proved time and again that it's not just some old myth. As the old story goes, the deeper the bond, the greater the distance the song can travel. I'm still glad your friend Boaz came to Kashmala when he did. I would have been a couple of hours later if he hadn't," Kavi explained.

"Boaz came to Kashmala!"

"Yes, he told me everything. I was surprised to learn that you had left. You usually let me know when you're about to travel."

"I'm sorry. I had a vision that was long and disturbing. I left to clear my head, and as I was traveling, I accidentally intercepted a message that involved Sheraga. Then things started spiraling out of control. I'm sorry, I should have told you and Zeroun."

"You didn't even tell Zeroun that you were leaving? I'm astounded," Kavi raised his eyebrows in disbelief. "Love, I know I can't understand the things you see, but you should have at least told Zeroun," Kavi gently reminded her.

"I know, I just got scared because of that long, disturbing vision . . . I think I killed him." Aqila started to cry. "I got scared and started searching for answers on my own even though I'm not a full seer. I almost threw my own life away."

"We can't avoid all mistakes in life. Some mistakes help us learn and grow into the people we are meant to become. Aqila, when we get back, you have to tell him everything. A part of his life's destiny is to help you. Your destinies are intertwined by the Universe, and you can't run from that. Now, I need to tell you that it is partly my fault that you got poisoned."

"What do you mean?"

"I made the poison some months ago. It wasn't supposed to be used on people. Chiefess Marina contacted me needing help with a whaling sanctuary the Beach Tribe is working on. I made a whale tranquilizer and sent it to her. Later she told me she never received it. I was confused about it, but she had deadlines, so I told her I would make another test batch and deliver it myself. In the testing phase, smaller animals showed signs of permanent paralysis. I made the antidote, and it removed the paralysis. That's how I had the antidote. I made it with the whale tranquilizer. The Snow Tribe must have intercepted it for their own use. I am still furious that someone decided to use my work to bring harm to you."

"It's okay, Kavi. The Waterbearer admitted that she didn't mean to give me as much as she did. I'm just thankful that the Universe was with us, and things were not any worse than they were. The person I reached out to being the one with the antidote was not a coincidence. And my bond with Talon is so strong, that he was already on his way to me."

"I know, I don't want to imagine a world where there's me without you." Kavi turned and kissed Aqila's forehead.

Aqila wrapped her arms around Kavi's waist and laid her head on his shoulder. She felt almost entirely like herself after taking the antidote. Her body was no longer stiff and hurting. She wanted to tell Kavi about Neptune and Agni. Still, she needed to gain insight into her visions to interpret the information accurately. She was tired from her ordeal but determined to ensure that Jai was all right.

"Oh, I almost forgot. I entrusted Boaz to deliver the message about the Legend's safety and the impending danger. It was the only way I could think to address two issues at once. I didn't want you to worry that nothing was being done about the death vision you were having."

"Thank you. At least for the moment, I can focus on these visions about Zeroun before I check on Jai," she sighed.

"I'm just relieved that you're okay. I worried about getting here in time. It's so absurd, like the entire Snow Tribe has gone haywire," Kavi explained.

"Well, besides Tiber and Nahal, there were only a handful of additional people. I wouldn't say that was the entire tribe."

Kavi scoffed, "Yeah, you only saw an additional handful of people. I touched down at the crack of dawn and spent the entire morning setting chemical gas traps to clear a way to get to you. Trust me, there were definitely more than a handful of people."

"I stand corrected. Now it makes sense why I didn't hear anything."

"Yes, the times when my sound abilities are most useful. You should have seen them. They never heard me coming. You know, they would try to yell and shout, and their fellow tribesmen couldn't hear a thing,'" Kavi smirked.

"Talk about advanced abilities. I didn't realize that I was using an unusual amount of oxygen until I stopped focusing on using it," Aqila reflected.

"I was going to ask how you did that," Kavi replied.

"Well, I separated the oxygen from the water and used it to stabilize my ability because my body had gotten so weak. I could not use any of my usual abilities. Then I realized that manipulating oxygen was another ability I could use. All the time, I didn't think I had a good mastery over the base element, but I did! I used it on Tiber. I was able to keep her from inhaling or exhaling with minimal effort."

Kavi laughed at Aqila's explanation. "What's so funny?"

"I was just thinking that down the line, we're probably going to have kids that have some crazy mash-up of abilities that are going to be mind-bending," he said, smiling at her.

"Well, if it is only a couple of them, I guess it won't be too unmanageable."

"A couple? We're going to have six or seven of them." Kavi smirked.

"What?"

"Yes, let's fill the Capitol with our kids.

"Um, no, let's not." Aqila raised an eyebrow before laughing at her fiancé.

"What? That's too aggressive, he chuckled.

"Way too aggressive," she laughed.

He sighed, "Official number to be determined later."

"Yes, to be determined." Aqila looked down at the scenery below. The grassy meadows of Wyndhm were lush and beautiful. The air smelled like a never-ending spring. Birds of all kinds took to the air. The sky was peppered with peaceful, wispy clouds, and a gentle breeze laced through the Windmasters' hair.

Kavi signaled for Sterling to land. Talon, who had been hovering not too far off the ground, followed Sterling's lead. "Stay here and relax for a bit. I'll take Talon to the sanctuary."

Aqila nodded as Kavi encouraged Talon to walk with him. They landed in the eastern part of Wyndhm. It was early, and many shops were just beginning to open. Aqila sat on Sterling, stroking her plumage carefully. A few young children could be seen in the distance, being sent off to school by their mothers. Some older children were wobbling on their dasher's backs, hovering only a few feet off the ground. One girl lost her balance and fell off her dasher, only to be caught in her father's strong arms. He held her close to him before encouraging her to try again.

Aqila sighed to herself. There was so much peace and happiness in Wyndhm and Kashmala. She loved her home.

Seeing the children with their parents made her wonder about her parents. This churned the fire to complete her seer apprenticeship. She wouldn't have these moments with them, but she was hopeful that they could share many other firsts. She was blessed to have another opportunity to fulfill her unique destiny and experience a life of complete happiness.

CHAPTER 14

Boaz could barely keep his eyes open as he rode Magma through Upper Ember. He turned to Sheraga, who appeared to have endless energy as he quickly guided his Komodo dragon throughout the region. They had been on the move all last night, not even stopping for a break. Having had a long and stressful day, Boaz was utterly worn out. As much as he wanted to rest, he understood the urgency of locating Jai.

He wanted to talk to Sheraga, but every time he thought of something to say, those intense amber eyes were all he could focus on. Sheraga physically seemed strong beyond his years. Although his wine-colored clothes and gold armor covered most of his body, one would have to be a fool not to notice that the DragonLord was all muscle. Something about the look in his eyes made one know better than to cross him. Boaz knew he was still in foreign territory, so he had to be cautious. Magma had been trailing behind Sheraga and his dragon the entire time. The sun lightly kissed the horizon, signaling the start of a new day.

Sheraga slowed to match Magma's pace, "You don't talk much," he flatly stated, never looking in Boaz's direction.

"What's there to talk about?"

"There's plenty to talk about. How do you know Aqila? What details did she give you about this death vision? What is her fiancé planning to do about her apparent disappearance? But you can start with, who the hell are you, and why should I be inclined to trust you?"

Boaz did not anticipate a firing round of questions from the DragonLord. However, everything he asked was reasonable. "My parents are librarians in Theyra. We live in a village in the Theyran Desert and own a landmark library. I work with my parents collecting, maintaining, and renting out books. Aqila's mentor, Zeroun, started bringing her to the library when she was young to study various topics. We became friendly, especially since we are so close in age. As we got older, sometimes Aqila would just visit to talk about her reading material. We would give each other book recommendations and talk about them later. I didn't know she was an apprentice seer until much later.

"When she came to drop off her books yesterday, she seemed a little off, like something was bothering her. She didn't go into details about her vision other than to say that the need to have a vision increased after leaving the area where Jai was. She said she was worried about having a death vision about him. Then she told me that she thought Jai was heading to Ember's border. Aqila didn't go into any details. The vision was becoming too strong."

Boaz then explained briefly, "I'm not sure what Kavi will do or how he will find Aqila. But, after meeting him in person, I do not doubt that he will find her and bring her back home safely." He was unsure how much information he should give Sheraga.

Sheraga shook his head, "Kavi is like a brother to me. I know he won't stop until she is safe. No real man just accepts that someone is out to harm the woman he loves. I just needed to know who I'm working with."

Boaz was nearly frustrated. He asked all of those questions for no apparent reason. Now, Boaz had a question for the DragonLord, "Why do you want me to come with you? I mean, you already know that tensions are high between Firehearts and Landkeepers. I don't see how I can be of any help to you."

"I don't expect you to be of much help either," Sheraga shrugged, "I brought you because if things did take a turn for the worst and Jai and some Flamethrower are injured, I'd be wasting time to make two trips. Since Tora needs to stay put, thanks to your kind of folk, I didn't have much choice."

Boaz felt offended. He really thought Sheraga believed that he could be helpful at some point. But in a perfect world, he would have chosen Tora instead.

Sheraga turned and looked at Boaz, "But I might be impressed to see you make yourself useful. We aren't too far from the border now. For the love of the Universe, it's bad," Sheraga groaned, shaking his head in anguish.

"What's the problem?"

"Can't you smell that?" Sheraga retorted sharply as if Boaz was ignorant.

Boaz inhaled and exhaled. He didn't know what Sheraga was talking about.

"Smoke and tons of it—let's get going. Ash, charge!" The Komodo dragon darted in the direction of the border.

Boaz shook the lantern near Magma's neck, "Come on, let's keep up." He was surprised at how quickly Magma picked up speed, especially since she moved slower the entire trip. The closer they got to the border, Boaz's eyes began to sting from the smoke. The thick substance made breathing somewhat tricky. He could barely make out Sheraga's red hair. The deeper he went into the smoke, the more lightheaded he became.

"Boaz, stop and let me clear the smoke some," Sheraga called to him, hearing Boaz coughing fitfully. Using his first two fingers, Sheraga quickly redirected the smoke in another direction. When the smoke cleared, Boaz should have felt sick to see all the blood and dead bodies, but he didn't. The smoke clouded the atrocious sight and the stench of blood-stained earth. Aqila's death vision had already come to pass. The entire area seemed deserted. The smoke rose from the ruins of a once-thriving village that now was nothing more than a scene of destruction and chaos. Every building was reduced to rubble, their charred remains smoldering in the aftermath of an unfortunate battle. The acrid smell of burning flesh filled the air, making it difficult to breathe. The smoke stung Boaz's eyes and coated his throat, leaving a bitter taste in his mouth.

"There's no one here," Boaz murmured.

"They probably all evacuated in the chaos of whatever battle happened here," Sheraga replied. "Arrow! It's your brother!"

"Jai! Is anyone alive?" Boaz asked, trying to keep his voice from cracking.

They both dismounted their reptiles, and Sheraga ran to a pile of ruins, removing the stones as fast as he could. "Sheraga, let me do that. It'll save some time." Boaz planted his feet in a wide-legged stance. He balled his fists tightly, keeping his elbows bent close to his sides, and lifted his fists. As his hands raised, so did the stones. As he turned his body to the right, he tossed the stones in that direction.

"You've made yourself useful already," Sheraga thanked the Landkeeper. Sheraga turned the heads of every single body under the pile of ruins and pulled one body aside. As he looked for survivors, Boaz continued to remove stones, uncovering bodies every time. Under one set of ruins, a black-haired young man fluttered his eyes.

"Sheraga! He's alive, look," Boaz pointed to the young man.

Sheraga ran toward him and called, "Flame! Come on kid." The teenager was coughing, gasping for air. "Flame, I'm going to pull you up," Sheraga lifted him with great ease. He gently placed him on the ground, laying his body straight out.

He's a kid? What on earth could have happened here?

Boaz heard more coughing and saw someone moving. He slowly stood up and gasped for air. Their eyes met, "Are you okay? I'm here to help," Boaz asked, extending his hand.

The red-haired man didn't accept it but looked past Boaz at Sheraga, "Sheraga, how did you get here?"

Sheraga stood and bolted toward his fellow Pyrocean, "Arrow, you okay, baby brother?" Sheraga extended his hand as Boaz had done, and Arrow immediately accepted, staggering over bodies as the pair embraced.

Suddenly, Arrow pushed away from Sheraga, pointing past them, "Yuuna and Beamer!" He stiffly hobbled toward a red-haired woman and a black-haired man who were not far off. Sheraga followed his brother, and Boaz continued looking for survivors. Arrow jumped back a few feet and covered his eyes.

"Arrow, calm down, let me look," Sheraga spoke.

"Beamer's dead, he's dead." Arrow shook his head feverishly.

He's never seen a dead man?

Sheraga checked his pulse, but there was none. Beamer's bright honey-colored eyes were still open, and his last expression was one of shock. Sheraga sighed, slowly closing Beamer's eyes. "Thank you for your service," he whispered into Beamer's ear. He reached out for Yuuna, and she stirred. Faint lilac scales pulsated underneath her eyes as they fluttered before rolling back into unconsciousness. He turned to his distraught brother, "Arrow, place Yuuna and Flame side by side on Ash." Arrow followed instructions without a word.

Beamer was a kid too. He could not have been much older than my siblings.

"Sheraga, they are alive over here, but one is bleeding out now that the stones are gone," Boaz called out. Sheraga hastily made his way to the three bodies Boaz had set aside. He recognized all but one. One of the twin girls was unconscious but clearly breathing.

"Jai!" Sheraga exclaimed.

Something unusual was going on. Sheraga placed his fingers on Jai's neck, his pulse was quick. Sheraga placed his ears near his chest and heard Jai's heart beating rapidly, "His heart is racing."

However, Jai was as still as a dead man. The other man was brown-skinned and appeared to be older than Jai. He had a large gash in his stomach which started to bleed profusely.

"Whoever stabbed him tried to do him in," Sheraga mumbled. "Boaz, there are some medical supplies in Ash's travel bag. Bring all of them to me. I need to stitch and wrap him up," Sheraga instructed.

Boaz ran to the bag and brought Sheraga everything he could find. "Keep looking for survivors with Arrow. Go a bit easy on him. Some of the deceased . . . were his friends."

Boaz saw Arrow walking mindlessly. His footsteps were heavy, each one carrying the weight of disbelief and sorrow. His amber eyes held a vacant emptiness as he moved among the lifeless forms of his friends. The air hung heavy with an unspoken grief, the silence broken only by the occasional choked breath or distant echoes of their footsteps. Boaz took a deep breath and headed toward him.

"Arrow, let's look over here," he pointed to a young man in an open area alone. They walked cautiously toward him.

Arrow froze, "It's Cahya. Could you check? I can't bring myself—"

"Yeah," Boaz checked his pulse; he was alive, "he's just unconscious. I'll place him on Ash like you've been doing." Boaz lifted Cahya and steadily walked to Ash. Arrow thought he heard something and walked toward the sound. The closer he got, he recognized the sound to be ragged breathing. Arrow moved closer to the survivor. A flicker of light came to his soul. It was Calida.

"Calida, Cal, it's me, Arrow," he called to her. He reached out his hand, offering to help her up.

She coughed, "I can't move anything but my head, Arrow."

Arrow's eyes went wide. He slowly dropped to his knees and patted her matted black hair, "What do you need me to do?"

"Tell me where I'm bleeding," she replied.

"Calida—"

"Please, Arrow, just tell me," she pleaded.

He sighed and touched her left side near her ribcage, "The back of your head and your left side— let me get Sheraga. He'll stitch you." He turned to stand.

"Arrow, Arrow, this is well beyond stitches," she whispered.

Arrow wiped the tears from his face, "Don't quit on me Calida! J— Just let him try. He can use Dragon—"

"Arrow, hold my hand, please," he took her small hand inside his, "I'm paralyzed, and I'm bleeding out. Please hear me, I only have time to say it once. I need you to lead them, the Flamethrowers. You must succeed me. This is a setback, but the mission must continue. Promise me that you won't let my family's legacy die. Promise me," tears started at the corners of her eyes.

"I-I promise. I'll protect your legacy, and I will lead them. Trust me, for you and everything you are to me, I'll lead them," Arrow vowed.

"Thank you." The tears fell from her face. Arrow used his free hand to wipe them away.

"I just wish I could save you," his voice cracked.

"Arrow, you did save me. Those three years have gone by so fast. You believed in me, my family, and our mission.

You fought for it like it was your own. You brought joy and happiness to my life that I would have never had without you. You fought for me and with me through so many obstacles for so many victories. You always freed me from anything that threatened to shackle me. You brought the Flamethrowers honor by leading Jai to us so we could continue our pledge to the Universe to support our Legend. All the things my parents taught me about love, I heard it all. But I really learned to love because you loved me. You made me a better person. I-I love you."

"I love you too." Tears from Arrow's face fell onto Calida's. He went to wipe them off.

"Don't! I can't even feel your hand right now. I just know that it's there. These tears are the last things I'm going to feel from you. " Her eyes began to flutter. "And be sure to take my necklace. Cyra gave that to my great-great grandfather, and my father gave it to me. Keep the legacy alive."

The pair sat silently for several minutes, gazing into each other's eyes. Calida's breath hitched; then she sighed, "I'll always love you, Arrow."

Arrow looked into her honey eyes. His lips trembled as he mustered a smile, "I love you too."

"Thank you for everything. And Arrow," she paused.

"Yes," he held his breath.

Calida mustered a smile, "Don't be afraid of anything that reminds you of me."

"I promise."

"Good, keep all of your promises," she smiled. Her last breath was a whisper before her honey-colored eyes became still. Arrow sobbed, squeezing her hand. He dropped his head into her neck and cried. In the hushed aftermath of Calida's final breath, he crumbled beneath the weight of grief as if his very essence had been fractured. His shoulders slumped, burdened not only by the lifeless form in his arms but also by the unbearable emptiness that was taking root within him. His hands, which had once lovingly held hers, now trembled with a mixture of grief and disbelief. Fingers that had intertwined so naturally with hers now hung limp, as if longing for her touch.

Sheraga watched his brother in the distance with a broken heart. Boaz came from behind him and looked at him hesitantly. Sheraga sensed his presence, "Leave him. He's not ready to let her go. He needs to have that moment."

Boaz nodded. Sadness crept into his heart watching Arrow cry over the body of the young woman he loved. He turned away, unable to watch. He did not know the feeling, and honestly, he never wanted to. He and Sheraga continued to search for survivors. Boaz could not help but feel for Arrow's loss.

Sheraga told Boaz that Jai, Alena, Cahya, Flame, and the man with the critical wounds were on Ash. Suvan, Yuuna, Kiran, and Arin were on Magma. Arrow staggered toward them, his eyes red and puffy from crying. He was wearing a thin chain with a ring on it. He was not wearing this before.

"I'll take Calida and Beamer and bury them in the Flamethrower gravesite deep in the forest. Where should I meet you later tonight?" he asked Sheraga. Sadness lingered on every word. He was lost in a world of his own grief. Tears streamed silently down his face as he mourned the loss of those dear to him.

"Meet me at Tora's house." Sheraga gently touched his brother's shoulder, "I'm sorry about Calida."

Arrow wiped his eyes once more. "Thanks, brother. I need to get going." Arrow walked away, finding a cart. He lifted Beamer's body into the back before gently lifting

Calida and placing her beside him. He put a chaste kiss on her forehead as he closed her eyes.

"Will he be okay going by himself?"

"Yeah, he'll be okay," Sheraga replied.

Arrow pulled the black hooded cape over his face.

Sheraga watched his brother with a heavy heart, then looked at all the bodies surrounding them, "Boaz, I'm going to stay back and bury them. I'll tie a fire light onto Ash, and he will follow Magma back to Tora's place. Go back exactly how we came, so no one sees you. You should get back sometime in the afternoon. Tell Tora that Arrow and I will be there by evening."

"I will. You can trust me." Boaz nodded.

Sheraga smiled, "I know. Thank you, go ahead and get going."

Boaz ran to Magma while he waited for Sheraga to set up the firelight. He attached it to Ash's neck and spoke some words. The Komodo dragon walked toward Magma.

"He's ready, go ahead to Tora's," Sheraga instructed.

"I'll see you later," Boaz called. He patted Magma, signaling for her to go. Boaz was off, riding a reptile with several unconscious bodies following him. He didn't expect this to be the outcome. Aqila went missing yesterday, and it was obvious that this attack happened at some point yesterday. Boaz felt frustrated. This is what he wanted to prevent.

Ila appeared before him. Her semi-transparent figure took a seat beside Boaz on Magma's back. "This is not the end. You were a valuable asset today."

"I don't feel that way. Maybe I was too slow. What if I took too long to get help? If only I had paid more attention, Aqila would have never been kidnapped. She could have saved them," Boaz looked away from Ila.

Another voice broke in. "As I see it, Sheraga would still be removing stones if it wasn't for you. The longer they stayed under the ruins, the less chance anyone had to survive. As Ila said, you proved to be a valuable asset." Basir appeared, "This event no one would have stopped from happening. Something was going to happen here yesterday. Maybe there could have been fewer casualties, but something was going to happen anyway."

"How do you know that?"

"I am irrevocably connected to the Seers, but now is not the time to tell that story. My connection to them is how I know these things," Basir answered.

"You are here for a reason Bo. The journey ahead won't be easy, but I promise it will be worthwhile. The longer and harder the battle, the sweeter the victory," Ila smiled. Just as they came seemingly from nothing, Basir and Ila disappeared. Boaz felt better after talking to them. They always came to him when he needed them most. For the first time, Boaz felt that everything was going to be okay.

CHAPTER 15

"I'll pick Talon up tomorrow afternoon," Kavi related to Aqila.

"Thanks, but if you're busy, I don't mind going to get him," Aqila replied, trying to be considerate of Kavi's work.

"My mind is already made, love. Your future husband will have everything taken care of." Kavi smiled. "Where do you want me to take you? Would you rather get some rest for a while or go home to Zeroun?"

"I feel I need to go home. I owe Zeroun my honesty and an apology before I do anything else. I won't have peace until I do," Aqila replied.

"All right then, I'll take you home. I'm proud of you. That was the best choice," Kavi sighed as the pair continued through the sky. The mountains of Kashmala were in sight. The tall, nearly impenetrable mountain chain was capped with clouds. It was a beautiful day. Sterling flew past the state's peaks to the far east of Kashmala's mountains. The Great Gray flapped with tremendous power as it pursued the highest peak of the eastern mountains. Sterling hovered over the peak, low enough for Aqila to quickly jump down.

"Thank you for everything, Kavi." Aqila lovingly gazed at him.

"Of course, love. I'll send Talon on his way once I pick him up. Now, take it easy, and at some point, try to rest." He reached out and gently stroked her hair. "I love you."

"I love you too," she whispered.

Kavi leaned in close to Aqila and gazed deeply into her silver eyes, "Next time, at least let me know when you're leaving like you normally do," he whispered, tilting her chin upward.

"I will." Aqila reached out and gently touched his face.

"All right, I'm off." He patted Sterling on the neck, and she began to lift higher into the sky. Aqila watched until

Kavi and Sterling were out of sight, flying into the depths of the clouds.

She sighed. It had been a while since she had spent time with Kavi. She was beginning to miss him already, down to the subtle smell of ink that laced his clothes. She turned to the house on the mountain. It was made with medium-sized off-white stones. The roof was made with slabs of bluish-gray slate complimenting the light blue door. Delicate plants and shrubbery surrounded the house. The size was not large nor too small; a family of four could quickly call this home, and for two seers, it was perfect. Aqila walked forward, steeling her nerves, ready to account for her actions.

The moment she was about to knock, the door opened. Before her stood a seven-foot-tall man with dark gray eyes and white curly hair. His deep golden brown skin appeared to be in its late seventies, but Aqila knew he was already three hundred years old.

"You've returned, my esteemed pupil." He smiled at her with gentle eyes.

"Yes, I apologize for leaving without conferring with you first. I know that I should not have done that." Aqila looked Zeroun in the eyes.

"Young master, follow me now. You're right on time." Zeroun stepped outside, closing the blue door behind him. Aqila obeyed her mentor and followed him closer to the mountain's edge. He sat down with his legs folded, and Aqila swiftly followed her mentor's lead.

He sighed, "The fresh air is sublime. Now, what was it that you were trying to say?"

Aqila smiled gently, "I was apologizing for leaving the way I did. I had a disturbing vision and wanted to try and clear my head from it. My journey ended up being bittersweet. I met the Fireheart Legend, and we spent some time together. However, I also was captured by a Snow Tribe girl . . . and almost lost my life. I was paralyzed, and the only thing I could think of was that if I died, I would have wasted your time. I was frustrated with myself, and I still am. Even a Waterbearer knew that I was a pitiful seer for getting caught like that."

"Aqila, you're still young. Don't be so hard on yourself."

"I can't help it. That was one of the dumbest things I've ever done! I'm supposed to be a seer! I'm a Windmaster! I'm supposed to be intelligent enough not to get captured."

"Experience is the mother of wisdom. The important thing isn't that you were captured. The important thing is you survived."

Aqila sighed deeply as she began fiddling with her hands in her lap.

"What was this vision about that brought such unusual character out of you?" Zeroun reached for her hands, "Why don't we look together."

Aqila pulled her hand back, and her heart almost stopped. She did not want her mentor to see what she had seen, "I'm sorry. I'm too embarrassed to show you." She hung her head down.

"Why? Because I die?"

Aqila's breath caught in her throat, afraid of how much her mentor knew. Then Zeroun started laughing, "It's not funny! I-I," Aqila started.

"I already know what you saw and what it means," Zeroun said, catching his breath.

"You already knew about it?" Aqila turned away, embarrassed. She felt like an even bigger fool for running.

"Aqila, my time has come. You shouldn't be afraid of that. My time has come, and so has yours. This moment, right here, is going to transform your life—this is the moment you become a full seer," Zeroun explained.

"Really? I-It's my time?" Her silver eyes beamed with happiness as she placed her hand over her heart.

"Yes, like in our studies, there can only be one seer. You have had limited vision, but this changes today. The moment you were born was the last time I could see into the future. And heavens, I laid asleep for days, unable to move from where I lay, with the sight. I knew you had been born at that moment. The Universe showed me what you looked like, the sound of your voice, and little glimpses into your life. As you got older, your sight for the future strengthened, and mine weakened. So much so that now I can only see the future through direct physical contact with you. A full seer must be able to see the past and the future. You could never see the past because I had that sight. I stopped seeing the future because you gained that sight. Therefore, the only way for you to become full is if I die and pass the sight of the past to you."

Aqila's eyes watered, "That's the only way? But I still need you. Why do you have to leave me," she sobbed. Zeroun lovingly wiped her eyes dry.

"Think of this, if everyone at the beginning of time were still alive, we would have never lived. Now, I could have dragged this out, as most have done. It is not a thirty and fifty-year-long process to become a seer. A terrible teacher could have a pupil ready in twenty years. It took so long because the past seers were afraid of this moment. They didn't want to die. But that keeps the student from living their life. You want to meet your parents, get married, and fulfill your potential. I don't want to keep you from that. I have to pass the torch to you."

"What happens when I need you?"

"That's why you need the sight of the past, to reflect on everything I have taught you. You can go as far back in time as your mind's eye is strong enough to travel. Trust me, you will have more information and lessons embedded into your brain than you will ever need. Twenty years ago, the Universe revealed how unique you would be. You had to go through that ordeal in Avala to glimpse your true potential. The vision of the circle divided into four equal parts is a Legend vision—to tell you the identity of the Legends."

Aqila's eyes went wide, "But, the one with the Windmaster stopped at you! How is that possible?"

"It stopped at me because I am still the seer. It was a hint that the Windmaster Legend is you, a seer. It has always been you. The Universe showed me twenty years ago. You came into power because of your ordeal. I have been blessed to have lived in the lifetimes of two Legends. I must say, you were everything Basir prayed for you to be. This is why I must go. The Fireheart has awakened. He needs you. The world needs you. Your strength, wisdom, and fearlessness are needed, Aqila. My life's purpose was to prepare you to face your destiny. The Heavens favored you for a reason. Long after you're gone, the Windmasters will know your name."

The Heavens favored me . . . I'm not even sure if this is what I want for my life.

CHAPTER 16

He looked at Aqila, who was as still as a statue, "Are you all right?"

"I think so," she shifted, "my best is all I have to give. If the Universe chose me, who am I to refuse the call? I just feel bad about wishing for my training to end. Now, it's staring me in the face, and I feel like I need more time just to be your student."

"Turn, Aqila, so that our knees are only a few inches apart."

"I can't do this!"

"You can. You must. Lightly form a fist with both hands and bring your hands to your chest. Never hold your breath. Focus on your mind's eye. I will talk you through everything that is going to happen." The pair closed their eyes. Aqila could hear Zeroun talking to her using his mind's eye, "Focus on your mind's eye. Can you see me?"

Speaking through her mind's eye, she replied, "I can see you."

"Good, now we are in the back of my mind, and we will talk and travel to the front. Once we get to our destination, your mind will be ready to receive the sight of the past."

It seemed as if the pair were walking a pathway lit with a bright white light. Though physically sitting with their legs folded in Kashmala, in another space, they were operating entirely through their mind's eyes. Aqila walked beside her mentor, torn between curiosity and sadness.

"I know you may not know what to say, but I want to take the last of my time to tell you that this partnership has been a highlight in my life. You were so young when I came to retrieve you from the Azure Temple. You resisted your destiny with such rage and determination. But in time, you grew into everything you were meant to be. Now, you have blossomed into a remarkable young woman. I am thankful that your parents shared you with me."

"This has been an incredible journey. You've given me so much love and care to pair with the wisdom and training to become a seer. I do not know my parents, but you were likened to a father and mother figure. You were everything I needed, exactly when I needed it. I am thankful for you. I'm a little worried. I have never heard of a seer being a Legend as well. This would not have been a path I chose for myself. I would have been content with a much simpler life."

"The Universe knows what's best for us, Aqila."

"I understand that now. When I was in Avala fighting with Tiber, I felt like something was happening to me. Something that I didn't understand— I can't put a name to the feeling."

"That poison would have killed any other. The only way for you to recognize your place in the grand scheme of things was to take your mind off of being a seer. Once you did that, other abilities that you always had welcomed the freedom to come forth in great magnitude," Zeroun explained.

"I could *always* separate oxygen by itself and manipulate it?"

"Yes, to be honest, many Storms can do that. They just never pushed the ability to its limit. Aqila, you would run outside in the rain when you were younger and then come inside and "shake" yourself. You would be dry afterward. You always thought it was from shaking, but you were pulling the oxygen from the water. You never noticed you were doing that. As I said, that ability is not unusual among Storms. You are actually the second Storm to be a Legend."

"Yes! I am! The Woman of Red, Storm of the Red Clan, she was the first Legend who was a Storm; our ability is named after her!"

"Quite correct. She came before Basir and really shook things up for the Windmasters. But the Universe blessed us with her. There would not be a WindGuard without her. Aqila, I know you're worried about being a Legend, but don't be. As long as you continue to seek guidance through the Universe, your legacy will be a great one."

"Zeroun, how come I'm afraid of death? How come you're not? We are walking here, and we both know this is the end. You are ready to go, and I want you to stay." Aqila's eyes began to water again at the thought of her mentor dying.

"You know how we always talked about people being afraid of what they don't understand. This is one of those things. Now, you should be worried about doing something unintelligent and prematurely ending your life. But, once you have reached your purpose and it's your time, death is nothing to fear. Death is a part of life. It comes at life's end. I have lived three hundred years and learned and enjoyed the journey.

"Today is the end of the physical me. My body has expired. I have touched many people through having visions. I will live on through the things I have done in this lifetime. The spirit of me will live on through my deeds. Now, as seers, our lives are unique. Once I die, you will have access to all of my memories. It will feel as if a part of me is still vividly here. I am dying for you to live. We come from the earth and return to the earth. We live because others died, and we die for others to live. If you look at it spiritually, you will understand the purpose of death like you understand the purpose of life."

"Did your mentor teach you this?"

Zeroun smiled and closed his eyes, "This lesson Basir taught me. I was around your age when Basir went into exile. He was like an older brother to me. I admired him for his wisdom. He was wise beyond his years. That's what he was known as, Basir the Wise. When his exile was set, I was the one who ensured that he could communicate through letters. I wished to talk to him and tell him that I had visions about his future, but due to his exile, I could not. So we wrote to each other all the time. I read the sign in the Stars that the Universe had forgiven him. He was approaching forty years old at the time. He thanked me for reading the stars.

"Just when I didn't believe that one could be so enlightened, he had evolved immensely through his exile. His wisdom only deepened. He would visit my mentor, his great-grandmother, quite often. And we grew very close. He was a great mentor to me. I trained with my mentor, Veda, for thirty years. I was disheartened by her death. I, like you, was ready to live but not ready for her to no longer be a part of my life. Basir taught me about the cycle of life and death to this degree. He compared life to the moon, its waxing, and waning. We don't see the new moon, but that doesn't mean it's not there. When the physical life dies after having grown full, the spiritual life takes on a new birth, a new moon, in the lives of the people we touch."

"When you talk like that, it is comforting and inspiring. I don't feel that dread anymore," Aqila reflected.

"That's how I felt when Basir explained it to me. He would say, 'You will still have emotions and miss them, but you don't have to stay in a state of grief. The one who passed would have wanted you to keep living as if they were still beside you.' When Basir passed about seventy years later, I took those words and etched them into my soul. I rose every day to see what the Universe would send my way, taking on everything as if he was still with me. He was much older than me, but after my wife, he was my best friend." A single tear dropped from Zeroun's face.

"That's something special. Your friendship literally has surpassed a lifetime through me," Aqila exclaimed. "I am the successor of you and Basir. I'm honored to be here right now, learning the Universe's lessons while accepting the torch you are passing to me. I'd be grateful if I could learn, grow, and evolve into a fraction of anything likened to you. You took my dismay and showed me where a blessing was laid and how to be thankful for it."

"In the Universe, nothing exists without purpose—not life, not death, nor any of us. You are the first seer to ever be a Legend. Why? I really do not know. However, it is not my job to know. That is for you to live and discover for yourself." Zeroun chuckled, "I guess we are going to have to call you something other than just Aqila the Seer."

"I guess so," Aqila smiled wide, "what about Aqila the Seer and Windmaster Legend?" They eyed each other for a few moments trying not to smile. Suddenly, the pair burst into laughter.

"That's a little on the long side. I think people will fall asleep as soon as you say and . . ."

"I guess you're right. So what would you suggest?" she raised her eyebrow at her mentor.

"Hmm, I need to think about it some more." The pair continued to walk in silence. Aqila wasn't sure how far they had traveled or what part of his mind they had reached. After talking to Zeroun about what would happen, she felt less afraid of the future.

"Feeling better now?"

"Yes, I am not afraid anymore." This was the truth. Still, Aqila knew she would greatly miss her mentor's physical presence. The brightly lit pathway began to dim, and she knew they were nearing the front of Zeroun's mind and the end of him.

"I'm glad that I was able to say something that eased your mind. This is not an easy plight. The best things in life never are. However, they are always worthwhile. Well, here we are. We have reached the point where I end, and you begin." He turned, looking Aqila in her silver eyes. "Thank you, Aqila. Your very existence has taught me so much. You love, and you fight without fear. This has been a remarkable experience. Thank you for sharing my last years with me."

Aqila swiftly pulled Zeroun into a hug. She felt his chin on her head. Although they were in their mind's eyes, she could hear and feel the soft beating of his heart as if they were in the physical world. "Thank you, Zeroun. I love you so much, and I'm going to miss you. I promise to do my best, so your sacrifice will be worthwhile."

Zeroun let her go and gently patted her head. "I know, Aqila. I know." He clasped his hands onto hers, and his eyes began to glow. "My last lesson for you is this, the only way to truly die is to be forgotten by those you love. In the physical sense, this is farewell, my dearest Aqila the Legend Seer."

His eyes began to glow white, and Aqila felt a crashing wave of energy throughout her mind's eye. It was unlike anything she had ever experienced before. She felt her physical eyes burning as if they had been set on fire. She saw images, faces, and time periods that she had never seen before. Her hands trembled inside Zeroun's. It took every ounce of strength and discipline not to let go and run from the sensation. However, she steeled her nerves and held on. After several minutes, Zeroun disappeared from her mind's eye. Aqila felt another presence with her, but it was not her mentor.

"So you are the new seer." A thunderous voice called to her.

"I am Aqila the Legend Seer. Who are you? Where are you?"

"I am Emet the First Seer. I've been eager to feel your energy. The wisdom of a seer and the piercing power of a Legend. I'm impressed. Your mind's eye is not strong enough to reach me, for you would have to look to the beginning of the Universe to find me. However, what your eyes cannot see, your mentor has groomed your mind to focus on and understand. You are now a full seer."

"Air, in the physical sense, is the breath of life. Our element reigns the mind, and our purpose is that of truth. As a seer, you have the power to reveal the truth to those who seek it. You were born with the sight of the future. Zeroun has gifted you with the sight of the past. As you apply events of the past to the present, your future sight will grow by leaps and bounds. We are all with you.

Every seer who has ever held the torch, you have access to their memories. When your consciousness returns to the physical world, you may feel alone. As the first seer, I am here to reassure you that you will never be alone."

Aqila opened her eyes. She was no longer in the realm of her mind. Her consciousness had returned to the physical world. She took notice of the sky and the prickling of the green grass. She was no longer in the mental realm.

Zeroun was still sitting with his legs folded like hers. Suddenly, his unconscious body fell forward. Aqila caught him and carefully laid his body out on the ground. The reality of her mentor's passing hit her. She wiped the tears that fell from her face. She felt an image pressing in her mind's eye. It was of her and Zeroun and their last laugh before Aqila became the Legend Seer.

She sighed, "Everything's going to be alright." She looked to the clear sky and sighed again before walking toward the house to prepare Zeroun for burial. She knew the ritual she had to perform. He would be buried in the valley. And one week later, she would etch her name in the Book of Seers in the Azure Temple.

Midday came quickly as Aqila completed preparing Zeroun's body. She had covered him in salt and let him stay in the salt for an hour before wrapping his body tightly in linen and cloth bandages. Her movements were deliberate, guided by a mix of reverence and aching sorrow. The weight of responsibility settled on her shoulders, pressing down as she navigated the sea of expectations and rituals that lay ahead.

Her silver eyes, usually bright with curiosity, were now veiled with grief as if the light within her had been dimmed by the sudden loss. Yet, through the fog of tears, a steely resolve shone, fueled by the need to honor the legacy of her beloved Zeroun who had guided her path. She moved with a sense of purpose, meticulously laying out the intricate white garments that would accompany her mentor on this final journey.

Aqila proceeded with her plans to bury Zeroun. All seers were buried together in the Valley of Truth. She would not have Talon back until tomorrow, so Aqila drew her plan for a proper burial for her mentor. Time seemed to drag on forever as she went back and forth from feeling okay to fighting back the tears. She let her day pass her by, unable to find anything within herself to push her forward. As much as she did not want to feel sadness, she could not keep her heart from feeling a little lost in a world without her mentor.

Aqila immediately became alert to the sound of wings flapping nearby. She smiled a bit, recognizing a familiar Great Gray and Harpy Eagle. The winged creatures made a graceful landing at the edge of the mountain.

"Aqila! You're safe." She was immediately enveloped in the strong arms of Saar.

"I wasn't intending on bothering you, but Saar insisted on seeing for himself the evidence of your safe retrieval." Kavi walked over, pushing his brother away.

"Thank you," Aqila whispered, unable to make eye contact with either of them.

"What's wrong?" the brothers asked in unison.

Aqila wiped her eyes, "Zeroun passed this morning." She choked on her sobs.

Kavi gently pulled her into him and held her close, stroking her hair in an attempt to comfort her, "I'm sorry, love. I didn't know. Was he unwell?"

"No, it was time for him to pass and let me become the seer," she whispered.

"I'm sorry, Aqila. Is there anything we can do to help?" Saar asked, his eyes brimming with concern.

"If possible, I need to take him to the burial site today."

"Well, I can see that you're in good hands, and this really wasn't a good time for catching up. I'll head back if you two are okay. You both know where to find me if I'm needed. My condolences, Aqila."

Kavi nodded, signaling for his brother to head off. "Where's his body?"

"In the house," Aqila replied absent-mindedly. Kavi went inside. Moments later, he carefully carried Zeroun's body and placed him onto Sterling.

"I don't want to interfere with the tradition. Should you be taking this journey alone?"

Aqila swallowed hard before nodding.

Kavi walked over to Aqila and cupped her face. "Take Sterling so you can properly bury your mentor. I'll catch a ride with Saar. You can bring her back to me whenever you're finished. I will be at the Capitol. You're not alone, sweetheart."

"Thank you." Aqila looked down.

Kavi gently lifted her chin. "Anytime." He planted a loving kiss on her forehead as he ran his finger through her hair. He sighed a long sigh before briskly walking to catch up to Saar, who was about to leave on his Harpy eagle. The brothers waved at Aqila before leaving her mountainside home. Once they were no longer in sight, Aqila took a deep breath and dried her eyes before mounting Sterling, ready to take the long journey to the Valley of Truth. As the gentle wind danced through her hair, she heard Emet's voice.

We are always with you.

I know, but I can't help but miss him. I didn't think my heart would hurt like this.

I never expected you to feel nothing. It would be ignorant to think that your heart would not hurt. However, you will find peace once you have returned him to the earth, and once you have obtained peace, your heart will heal itself.

She took a deep breath as Sterling carried her and Zeroun to the valley.

CHAPTER 17

Boaz carefully made it back to Tora's house without being seen. He returned Magma and Ash to the backyard, where he was immediately greeted by Tora.

"That looks bad. Let's hurry and get them inside." He rushed toward Magma, lifting a body from her back. Boaz could easily lift two to Tora's one, and the pair quickly moved everyone inside. When they looked at Zay's bloodied body, both were hesitant to touch him.

"I'll grab his arms. You take his feet," Boaz suggested.

"I'm not even sure if we should touch him at all. Look, he's bleeding through the bandages. I'd hate to do more harm than good," Tora replied.

"Yeah, and if someone sees that you have a heavily wounded Fireheart in your backyard, that won't go too well for you either. Now help me."

Tora sighed heavily before aiding Boaz in carrying Zay inside.

"Let's take him upstairs with Jai. We can put him in my guest room," Tora suggested as they started inside. Quickly but carefully, they took Zay upstairs and gently laid him on the guest bed. "I have some medical supplies in my main bathroom. Stay here while I go and get it," Tora rushed out of the room.

Boaz closed the dark red curtains in the room. As he pulled them together, Tora reentered, "What are you doing? Scared of the light?"

"No, I just didn't want to take a chance at someone seeing what's going on here," he replied. "Something moved downstairs."

"I didn't hear anything," Tora shrugged while unwrapping Zay's bandages.

"I didn't hear anything either, but I felt something move downstairs. I'll go look," Boaz left Tora tending to Zay.

He carefully crept downstairs, not wanting to startle anyone. He heard murmuring voices. As he turned the corner, a few of the Firehearts had regained consciousness.

"Who are you?" a light brown-eyed girl with a dimpled right cheek asked.

"Boaz of Theyra, I helped Sheraga rescue you. Are you okay?" He slowly walked toward the girl before someone put him in a chokehold from behind. Boaz reflexively squatted and thrust his elbow into his attacker, sending him flying.

"What the hell is your problem?"

His attacker was large and sturdy, an unusual build for a Fireheart, "Where are we, and where is the Legend?" he asked, glaring at him, a bright fire manifested within his hand. Boaz jumped back as he saw a bright flash from the corner of his eye.

"You're in my house, and the Legend is upstairs, you oversized fool." Tora walked downstairs, lightning flashing around his body like armor. Once he turned the corner, all the Firehearts went silent. His presence and power radiated off the walls of the room, lowering the heads of the group of bold and boastful Firehearts.

"Flamethrowers, huh? Well, you should be ashamed of yourselves. Talk about biting the hand that fed you."

The girl with the dimple looked with pleading eyes, "Tora of Kindle, please forgive us. We're sorry, we were just a little disoriented and shocked to not be in Ember. Where's Jai? Is he all right?"

Tora turned away from them, "I don't know, I'm no doctor, but I have dealt with my fair share of injuries. His condition is unusual, and I'm not sure what happened to him. I intend to wait it out until Sheraga returns. He's more well-versed in these things than I am. No one goes upstairs unless you plan on getting through me. Boaz, come on," Tora commanded.

"Can't you just get another doctor?" Arin pleaded.

"No, I can't, there's too much going on with Agni to risk it. He wouldn't be in the company of Flamethrowers if he wanted the world to know his identity."

"But what if he stops breathing or something?" Arin was clearly upset.

"That's the least of our worries; maybe I should clarify. Jai is stable for the moment. If he were to stop breathing, I'd give him a jolt."

The younger Fireheart was not thrilled with Tora's decision, but she didn't argue.

Boaz followed Tora upstairs to the guest room where Zay was resting. "I'm sorry about that. I should have stopped you from going down there. You're a Landkeeper. They were bound to be hostile. Look, I'm going to stay with the Legend until Sheraga returns. You stay here with him."

"Really, Tora, it's not like he's going anywhere," Boaz groaned.

"Whoever did this to him wanted to end him painfully and miserably. He was stabbed straight through the back and his back was badly burned. I'm shocked he's even alive at all."

"The rocky ruins must have kept enough pressure on the wound to prevent much blood loss."

"Must have. Either way, stay here." Tora turned and left the room.

CHAPTER 18

Downstairs, all of the Flamethrowers had awakened.

"Where's Beamer?" Yuuna asked, concern evident in her amber eyes.

"I don't know, but where's Arrow and Calida?" Flame asked.

"Don't know, but didn't that Landkeeper say that Sheraga helped rescue us? Maybe Arrow and Calida are with Sheraga," Arin said in a reassuring voice. She looked at her sister, her eyes distant and glassy. "Alena, it'll be okay." she scooted closer.

"It's all my fault."

"Don't say that." Arin touched her shoulder only to be violently swatted away.

"Shut up! Agni attacked Jai. He's fighting for his life because I couldn't stop him! Fiery arrow after arrow, and Agni burned them to ashes without looking my way! I was useless, and two people might die because of my failure. I let Agni get away—" Alena quickly wiped her tears away before hugging her knees.

"Two people?" Arin questioned.

"No, Alena, I let Agni get away. The building came down, and Calida went to attack Agni with all her might. He bested her, and I went at him with all my might. He was powerful. His element was unrelenting. I could not even sense the source. I can't tell if he was sourcing from the sun or his willpower. I thought I had him. I felt just a little give, and I tried to exploit it. When he blasted me back, I realized he wasn't even trying. In truth, I was no match at all. I let him get away. I was the last one to see him." Cahya trembled at the horrid memory.

"We have to stop talking like this." Suvan stood up, "We are all going to make ourselves feel like the biggest losers on earth if we keep this up."

Alena groaned, "Well we are."

Suvan shook his head, "No! We were outnumbered, and that's all. If only you had seen yourselves. This mighty little group thwarted the makings of an army. We're some fearless fighters. We are strong, talented, and brave. I saw each of you fight the biggest battle of your lives just now. We knew going in that it wasn't going to be easy. But this is not the end. We accomplished a part of our mission. We freed Sitara. Our Legend is fighting for his life. Why are we beating ourselves up to the point of giving up? We don't know if everyone made it out with their lives today, so we won't stop fighting. We will stop crying, sulking, and hating ourselves, right now!"

"I'm more surprised that Sitara didn't help us," Yuuna murmured.

"What do you mean? She couldn't stay, you know she has to complete her own undercover missions," Cahya replied.

"Maybe, but could it have hurt for her to help us? It may have been that extra boost we needed," Yuuna continued.

"Yuuna, we needed more than just an extra boost to have won," Arin added.

"Yeah, Agni alone was just too strong for us. Then who knew that he had that big of a following?" Alena spoke.

"It seems like his main following is Lower Ember. Most of them were giftless," Kiran chimed in. "Giftless, with deadly hand-to-hand combat skills and military formations."

"The ones guarding Sitara were gifted though," Yuuna said.

"What about you, Yuuna? Are you supposed to be a Pyrocean? You're supposed to be a dragon! You weren't too helpful. I couldn't tell that you were a Pyrocean at all," Kiran spat.

Yuuna's jaw dropped. "What do you mean?" Her lilac scales began to glisten.

"Enough!" Arin yelled. "Can we just stop? We have more pressing things to be concerned about! Think about Jai! Think about Arrow! Think about Calida! We don't have time to ignite flames against each other. Sitara is free to do the mission which in turn helps us as well. Everyone fought their hardest, everyone! So please let's just have peace," Arin said.

Everyone lowered their heads in agreement.

Boaz was upstairs listening to the bickering downstairs, wishing that things were different. He was sitting on the floor not far away from Zay. The room reeked of fresh blood as it stained his new bandages.

If only I had checked on her, maybe I would have seen her attacker.

He recalled the smell of smoke and blood on Ember's border, the subtle pain on Sheraga's face, Arrow's grief, and he wished he could have taken it all away.

"Why do you persist with thoughts like this?" Ila appeared before him.

"I know everyone has told me this was not my fault, but if not mine, then whose? I have this supposedly great destiny ahead of me, and I keep feeling like the most useless person on the planet. Going to the border and seeing all those bodies . . . that was normal for me. I walk through Theyra every day, and that's all there. It didn't hit me that it wasn't normal until I saw Sheraga and Arrow's pain. Sheraga looked like a commander who had lost his best soldiers. And he was honorable enough to stay back and bury every single person who died. Arrow grieved over the loss of his friends. And I didn't feel anything. That scene wasn't new to me. I don't want to be like that, Ila. How can I fulfill my destiny if I'm immune to the atrocities of the world I live in?"

"Bo, you're living in the aftermath of the problems I didn't fix. You have a great destiny. It's just hard to see through the dense shadows of my legacy. Listen to me, the Landkeeper's problem is that we hate change. We get used to things as they are and fight to keep them that way. We try to be immovable and fixed."

"Being determined, stable, and fixed has its strengths, but too much of anything can be negative. People cannot survive without change because they won't grow. Until the Landkeepers as a people learn the benefits of change, there will always be war. You have already mastered what most of our people, including myself, never did. You don't see a problem with something a little different from you. You befriended Aqila, took a chance, and went to Kashmala on her behalf. You flew through the sky into enemy territory to fulfill a mission. Boaz, you are far from useless, but you won't be happy saving others until you reach back for your own. The best practice is to help your own before helping others. Our people need you. I need you."

Her gentle moss eyes began to fade along with the rest of her. He felt better after talking to her. Out of the four, Ila's presence always comforted Boaz. Cyra never showed herself. Basir was understanding and factual. Aenon asked many questions and could be rough around the edges; however, Ila was like a friend and a guide. However, her presence weighed on him the most. He felt someone approach the door.

"Were you in here talking to yourself?"

"Yeah, Tora, I do that sometimes."

He leaned on the door frame while glancing back toward the room that Jai was resting in, "I can't imagine how things were on the border. All of them were unconscious. Jai and this guy are still out of it. Were Sheraga and his brother all right?"

"There were a lot of casualties. Sheraga stayed to bury the bodies, some of Arrow's friends passed, and he went to bury them in private. They said they would be back when they were done."

"I bet. You know, the crazy thing is that when this war is actually over, we may find it hard to exist without war."

"Well, as a people, we have all been waiting for peace for so long. We will nurture and protect the peace. We will fall in love with the idea of it and fight to the death to maintain it."

"I hope you're right, Boaz," Tora replied.

"How's Jai?"

"Stable, I guess," he sighed, "I haven't seen anything like this before. That's why I need Sheraga to return as soon as possible. So, I dressed his shoulder injury. He doesn't have a lot of wounds in that sense. But he's just not moving. His heartbeat is ridiculously fast, I'm worried for his heart. He is not responsive."

"Well, I'm not well versed in that kind of stuff, so I won't be too helpful." Boaz shrugged his burly shoulders. "I'm good with books, not medicine."

"There's nothing else we can do until Sheraga returns.

"What can Sheraga do that you can't? I understand why we can't get a doctor. Honestly, another doctor will probably hit the same block that you have. If his heart is racing, he could go into cardiac arrest, which you've already pointed out."

"I suspect poison is involved, Sheraga can use his ability and attempt to burn the poison from his system."

"What?"

"It's something called Dragon's Breath. It's like being covered in flames that won't burn. The purpose is to provide enough heat to force toxins to exit the body as it sweats."

"Then why not get the Pyrocean girl downstairs?"

"She's not strong enough. Did you see her scales?"

"What scales?"

"Exactly my point, she is not strong enough to do the technique. The more prominent the scales the stronger the dragon energy. Also, having the power to do it doesn't mean that one naturally has the skill for the technique. I need to check on Jai, let me know if he wakes up."

"Yeah, I will," Boaz affirmed as Tora returned to the room where Jai was resting. He hoped that Sheraga and Arrow would arrive soon. He didn't want anyone else to die today if it could be helped.

CHAPTER 19

Aqila sighed. She hadn't felt this level of relief in several days. It was early afternoon as she laid her beloved mentor, Zeroun, to rest. A wave of peace and purpose finally claimed her. Hearing a blaring screech, she looked up to the sky. The large wings of a dasher cast a shadow upon her.

Upon landing, she was pleased with the presence of the one who had arrived.

"How are you doing?"

"I'm feeling a lot better now, thanks Kavi." The pair briefly embraced before she gently brushed her fingers against Talon's feathery face. "I appreciate you making sure Talon was all right. He looks a lot better now."

"Anything for you." He sat in the lush green grass of the valley and ran his hands across the young green blades. Aqila sat down beside him and stared into the distance. "Ah! The Valley of Truth. I haven't been here in years. To be honest, I got turned around a bit. Are you really okay?"

Aqila's usually neat braid crown was messy, and strands of gray hair were wildly framing her face. Her bun was loose, the yellow hairpin was sliding free. Her hands trembled as they lay in her lap.

"I'm trying to be. I miss Zeroun immensely, and it hasn't even been a full day. I feel a little lost about everything I am now."

"What do you mean?"

Aqila didn't answer, she only hung her head. She clasped her hands and closed her eyes. Kavi sighed, gently leaning his shoulder into hers. Neither moved for several minutes. The silence was not awkward, but beautiful. Moments later, he placed a sweet kiss on her cheek, before turning her body so her back faced him. He pulled the hairpin free, then released the messy bun. Lastly, Kavi gently unbraided her hair. He ran his fingers through Aqila's hair to neaten it.

"Whatever it is, you can talk to me about it," he spoke softly as he redid her hairstyle.

Her silver eyes flickered nervously. She fidgeted with her hands, twisting and turning them as she prepared to speak her truth. "I'm not just a seer. I'm a Legend too. Zeroun knew the whole time about my vision, and he told me that I had to go through that ordeal in Avala to see my true potential. He said I was so focused on being a seer that I was not open to my true destiny. If this was just about becoming a seer, I would feel ready. I feel ready to be a seer, for the most part, but I'm unsure if I have what it takes to be a Legend. I've learned a lot about the previous Legends, and the truth is, it is not an easy role. It's a lot of responsibility."

It didn't take Kavi long to finish Aqila's braid and bun. After placing her hairpin back into the base of her bun, he smiled. He shifted so that he was sitting by her side, before stretching his tall body out with his head on her lap. Her silver eyes gazed sweetly into his as she weaved her fingers through his long straight hair, massaging his scalp.

"It is a lot of responsibility, and I can't imagine a better suitor for this destiny than you." He laid his head on her lap, looking straight into her silver eyes. "The

Universe chose you for this, they wouldn't choose you if you couldn't do it, and that is what I believe. Do you feel like this will have any negative repercussions?"

Tears fell down her face, "I-I have worked so hard! And every time I feel like I'm getting close to having my heart's desire, something threatens to take it away. I know I should not be selfish—"

"Aqila, it's okay to feel. Whether you are a seer or Legend, or whatever, you are still human. You have human feelings and emotions. And it's okay. Don't worry about what the future may bring. I'm here for you, supporting you every step of the way. Your destiny as a seer and a Legend only makes me love you even more. I am forever in awe of you." Aqila looked away and wiped her eyes. Kavi slowly sat up and reached out for her hand.

"I wasn't sure if you would be okay with this. I'm not even sure that your parents will still allow us to get married," she sobbed.

Kavi embraced her, "Aqila, I love you. It doesn't matter to me whether you are a seer or a Legend. If you were neither of those things, I would still love you. Even if I were a blind man, unable to see the most beautiful woman to grace this planet, I would still desire to marry you. You're more than a title. I'm in love with you, your mind, your thoughts, all of you. The way you think captures my entire being. Everything that is you cannot help but be enveloped by my love. I love your visions and every ability you possess. I swear on the Stars that will never change."

Aqila's sobs eased upon hearing Kavi's declaration of love. "I love you too."

"Nothing is going to happen to us. Before I left for Avala, I requested a leave of absence, and I reported to my parents when I returned. I learned that Zeroun had already visited them, explaining that he was about to pass the sight to you and make you a full seer. He also told them you were the Windmaster Legend and that your role would be different from any other seer before you. They sat me down and asked if my intentions of marriage were swayed by the revelation. I told them that my intentions remain resolute. Aqila, the wedding is still on."

Kavi brushed his fingers across her lips and then wiped away her tears, "They accept me as I am," she sniffled.

"Yes, they do. Now, that leaves us with one last quest before we can officially start our wedding arrangements."

"What's that?"

"Aqila, my dear, what kind of man would I be if I didn't receive your father's permission to wed you?"

"You're going to meet my parents?"

"No, *we* are going to your parents today, if you're up to it," Kavi smiled.

Aqila's eyes lit up, "Of course I am! Are we leaving now?"

"If you have wrapped things up here, we can go. I'm not sure when you have to do the next part of the ritual at the Azure Temple."

"I will go to the temple one week from today." Aqila looked back to the beautiful green valley. All the seers of the past were buried here. Once she passed on from the physical world, she would be buried here. Emet was right. She did find peace after burying Zeroun. She would forever miss his physical presence. However, he died so she could live. And for that, she was thankful. Breathing in the air, she felt comforted, reassured, and strong. It was an odd feeling knowing that one day she would be buried next to Zeroun. Her eyes never looked away from the tombstone she made. White marble, etched with the words, "Master Zeroun of three hundred years, successor of Master Veda and succeeded by Master Aqila." She was finally a master.

"I'm finished here. I'm ready," she replied.

The pair mounted their respective dashers and gracefully took flight into the Kashmalan skies.

"Do you know where my parents live?"

"On an isolated mountain at the border of Kashmala and Wyndhm. It's the same house that every seer's parents move to," he replied, the breeze weaving through his stone-gray hair. The pair flew in silence. Quiet is not necessarily a bad thing, but this was an awkward silence. Kavi and Aqila would periodically glance at each other from the corner of their eye, only to look away. They were both nervous about the meeting.

"Are you okay?" she asked Kavi.

"Yeah, I guess I'm a little uneasy. I'm going in with a big ask and I don't really know them. I barely remember them. I was three when you were born. I want to make a good impression. It's not like I have any pointers. I'm going to visit a couple who've been in isolation for twenty years to ask for their daughter's hand in marriage— the daughter that they don't even have a relationship with. Not to mention the fact that they don't know me either. It's a reasonable amount of pressure. I refuse to be the reason this relationship falls through."

"Trust me, I don't believe anything will fall through. I think they'll love you just as much as I do."

"Is that so? Then what are *you* so nervous about?"

"I don't know. I want them to like me for what I am. I don't want to disappoint them. They may have other children by now, and at this point, it may be impossible to create a bond with them. I've gone through so many firsts without them and want to experience things with them; however, realistically, that may not even be possible."

"Don't stress about it. Stressing about things is not the Windmaster way. We address things for what they are. I know it may be a little challenging. Yes, that's possible, but what if that's not the case? What if they see you and immediately want to bring you into the fold of their lives? That's possible too," he chuckled, "I guess we both have been getting a little worked up without a good reason. Why don't we focus on the present, do our best, and see how things go?" Kavi suggested.

"I agree, let's manifest positivity. By the way, how are your parents doing?"

"Busy as usual. They were heated about what happened to you in Avala. My father is rarely upset, so it was new to see him angry. They want to discuss next steps with the rest of the governing class. We don't want anyone else getting the idea that the sister states are fine with kidnapping our seer. Besides the Avala situation, things have been peaceful in Kashmala and Wyndhm. They are considering adding a university to Wyndhm because Kashmala's university is nearing max capacity. Wyndhm is on the fence about it. They seem to enjoy being the creative capital of the world."

"That's understandable. Their ancestry is mainly Yellow and Green Clans, so it's not unreasonable for them to dislike the idea of a school. Perhaps, it could be an opportunity for Wyndhm to secure its status as the creative capital with the a university focusing on the arts."

"I've considered that. I have also been thinking about a way to integrate the Red Clan in the mix."

"The Red Clan? Did not we already address that through the WindGuard?"

"It's the entire Red Clan we're talking about."

Aqila giggled at his remark. "Sounds like your parents will be busy for the rest of the year."

"Definitely! However, my mother is over the moon about the wedding, so she was borderline threatening me to make sure this goes well."

Aqila laughed, "It's the Storm in her! You know how much she loves weddings."

"Yeah, she does. Look up ahead. We're almost there," Kavi pointed to the mountain that was lightly covered in snow.

"So, this is where all seer parents go?"

"Yeah, this is where they all go. It's actually a nice place. It is huge with plenty of bedrooms and bathrooms, in case they have more children. And they are not confined here completely, they can travel to the first few towns in Wyndhm, but that's all." The pair landed their dashers on the mountain cliff. After dismounting, they slowly approached the off-white door of the mountainside home.

CHAPTER 20

"You want to knock?" Kavi asked.

Aqila slowly nodded and proceeded to knock on the door. They heard footsteps hurry to the door, then it slowly opened. A teenage boy stood in the doorframe. He had warm brown skin and light gray eyes. His ash-gray hair was short with loose curls. "Who are you?"

"I'm Kavi, Son of Akash and Sufa of Kashmala. Are Cirocco and Brisa of Kashmala available? We are here on state business." Kavi jumped to the point.

The teenager eyed them carefully. "Yes, come inside." Aqila and Kavi walked inside, taking in the cozy living area. "They are in the kitchen; wait here, and I'll get them."

The house interior was lovely, and the walls were light gray. The furniture was soft, off-white, and downy. The windows were large enough to allow substantial light in without a lamp. As they were observing the details of the decor, a man and woman entered. The man's complexion was rich golden brown. He looked about seven feet, six inches, with long dark gray hair and silver eyes. The woman was shorter than six feet by an inch or two. Her skin was warm, soft brown, likened to sugar cubes. Her ash-gray hair was pulled into a tight bun and fastened by a gold hairpin with an orange drop. They saw Kavi first, but when their eyes fell on Aqila, they quickly rushed toward her.

"Aqila? Is it really you?" Cirocco asked.

"Of course, I would know these eyes anywhere. My sweet baby girl," her mother cooed, gently caressing Aqila's face, her ash-gray eyes lovingly gazing at her daughter. They both embraced her. "Look at her. Isn't she just wonderful?"

Her father looked around, "Athens, come here," he called.

The teenage boy entered. "Yes, Father?"

"Meet your sister, Aqila," Brisa beamed.

Aqila waved at Athens. He awkwardly waved back, "Nice to meet you. So, being here means you've finished that seer training?"

"Yes, my training is complete, and I am a full seer."

Her mother wiped her teary eyes. Cirocco looked Kavi up and down, "So you're Kavi. I remember how small you used to be. You take after your father."

"Thank you. I get that a lot. My father and mother send their love and warm regards. Tomorrow evening they are hosting a private dinner for you to discuss your current and future living arrangements."

"That's incredible. I haven't spent time with your father and mother in such a long time. It would be our pleasure," Cirocco replied.

"Awe love, look, Aqila has a hairpin. Who's the special man?"

Kavi coughed abruptly. Aqila patted his back, "Are you okay?" she whispered.

He nodded. "Why the special man would be me. That was the state business that I needed to discuss with you."

Cirocco and Brisa looked at each other with raised eyebrows and looked back at Kavi and Aqila, eyeing them up and down. There was a slight frown on their faces.

She instinctively intertwined her hand with Kavi's, and he gently squeezed her hand. The pair stopped breathing for several moments. Had they done something wrong? Made a bad impression?

Aqila's parents burst into laughter. "Did you see their faces? They looked like they could have passed out on the spot," Cirocco bellowed.

Brisa was trying to catch her breath. "That was a classic. Remember how my parents did us? Don't worry, my dear Aqila, go spend time with Athens while we converse with Kavi." Athens proceeded to the door and motioned for her to follow him as he looked at her and Kavi's dashers.

"Nice, you have Great Gray owls. My dasher is a snowy owl, and her name is Winter. What are their names?"

"Talon is mine, Sterling is Kavi's," Aqila replied, "Are you going to school?"

"Yeah, I'm finishing my Associate in Horticulture Science, then I will resume my apprenticeship before going on to advanced studies. How about you?"

"Well, I started my seer training at ten, but I had finished Applied Astronomy by that time. I skipped a grade early on and finished the Applied program in a year."

"So my sister is a seer and crazy smart. I like it. How old are you?"

"Twenty, and you?"

"Sixteen, but I'm turning seventeen soon."

Aqila giggled to hear how excited he was for his upcoming birthday, "How do you like it out here?"

"It's nice, really. We don't get as much interaction, but I go to school in Kashmala, so that's nice. The state financially takes care of us. It's not like a complete exile or anything. So we never need anything. It's been awesome. We just didn't know how long it would take for you to finish. I heard it could take a really long time."

"Well, it varies depending on teacher and student," Aqila replied, reflecting on Zeroun.

"Who's the fiancé? You know you have to give me the details. He's not that tall, though."

"Please, he's average height, and you are literally only an inch taller." She playfully rolled her eyes.

"Taller is taller, and besides, I still have time to grow," Athens joked, "You think he's the one?"

"Without a shadow of a doubt."

"What makes you say that?"

"We have gone through so much together. We started school together. He's supported me through all the phases of my apprenticeship, the ups and downs. Actually, deciding to get married was a little scary. Kavi is in line to become the next ruler, so his parents, reasonably so, wanted to make sure we were serious—and prepared in case I could not finish my training within a reasonable timeframe. It was a lot of pressure, but he worked just as hard as I did for us to have a future together."

"That's nice. I could tell he was trying to protect you when I opened the door. I just didn't know why at the time. Well, this is a nice change of events. Mom and Dad always talked about you. In their hearts and minds, you were very much alive and a part of the family. They will be happy to get back to Kashmala. I think they like it here but are ready to return home."

"I want that for them too." Aqila smiled. "Athens, are you a Storm?"

"No, are you?"

"Yeah, I was just wondering."

"I know, but no father is a Storm. I inherited our mother's peaceful nature. So you're a seer, a Storm, anything else?" Athens joked.

"Well, actually, there is. I'm also a Legend," Aqila said.

Athens stopped and stared. "What? Is that even possible? You're a— the Legend of the Windmasters?"

"Yeah. I just found out, but that's our family secret."

Athens' eyes beamed. "The family secret is safe with me. Even though we just met, you're really awesome." Athens smiled.

"Aww, that means a lot to me. I really like you too. I was scared that I wouldn't fit in after all of this time. I wasn't sure if our parents had forgotten about me or if they had many other children and wouldn't have time for me. Seeing that I matter to you really means a lot."

"You know Mom and Dad were worried too. They said that a lot of times seers don't seek out their families after training. Their parents would just get a notice from the state that they are welcome to return home. I thought that was horrible, but Father said that your child doesn't know you at all. Depending on the state of things, they must fight to perform their duty to the best of their ability. It means a lot to us that you even made time to make the trip."

Aqila felt pressure behind her eyes and immediately began to see images flash before her. Never before had the sight come so easily, and it stopped her where she stood. She saw her paralysis in Avala, and then she saw a syringe before the images flashed to Jai at Tora's house.

Emet's voice was likened to a whisper, "Your experience could be helpful here."

The images ceased, and Aqila looked around to see Athens staring at her in disbelief, "You just had a vision! Your eyes got all bright and flashy. You were so still! What did you see? What did you see?"

"I can't tell you, Athens, but I need to prepare to leave," Aqila gently replied.

"Yes, ma'am! Duty calls!"

The siblings hurried back to the mountain house. They were met by Kavi, "Are you okay? I heard you talking."

"You heard us," Athens asked.

"Have you finished already?"

Cirocco and Brisa appeared, "Kavi sensed that something was up, and we decided to continue our discussion when we come to visit for dinner," her father replied.

"We have to go. It's urgent," Aqila expressed to Kavi.

"I figured. I'll prepare the owls. Cirocco and Brisa of Kashmala, it was an honor to be in your presence. I am looking forward to continuing our discussion." He bowed his head in respect before walking away.

Aqila walked up to her parents and hugged them. "I'm so happy to have met you and relieved to know that you missed me."

"Of course we missed you; we love you, and nothing will change that." Brisa reached upward to cup her daughter's face. Cirocco placed a loving kiss on her forehead as they embraced.

"Take care of yourself on your mission, Aqila. Love you!" Athens was grinning from ear to ear.

Aqila started for Talon. "I love you too," she whispered.

The pair were steadied on their dashers and proceeded to leave the snowy mountain in the farthest part of Kashmala.

Kavi eyed Aqila as they flew off. "So what's up?"

"Jai's in trouble at Tora's place. I have to go immediately. I hate missing the dinner your parents planned." She covered her face with her hands.

"They'll understand. Just be careful. If I was in position, I would accompany you. However, that is not the case."

"I'll be careful, I promise. Just to ease your mind, I will gather some medical supplies in Wyndhm before I set off."

"You won't need to. Just wait for me at the border. I'll bring some of what I have. If you're pressed for time, it will save you a trip in the opposite direction."

"I appreciate it. Kavi, were things going well . . . with my parents?"

He sighed a long, heavy sigh. "I'm not sure. I would like to think that things were going well. I was expecting more questions about our plans, but they were asking more questions about me and my future role as ruler. It was somewhat unusual. But I won't get an accurate feel of things until they have dinner with my parents."

"Why were they questioning your plans for rulership? I mean, there's a governing class with a ruler who makes the final decision based on the findings of the governing class. The ruler is accountable for the final decision and its outcome. From what I have been told, my father was once a part of the governing class; he knows how it works. So what does that have to do with our marriage?"

"Aqila, it could have everything to do with our marriage in your parents' eyes. I do realize that our roles could affect our future and the future of the Windmasters.

A ruler and a seer have never been married before. A ruler and a Legend have never been married before except when Aenon married Avala. And we know how that turned out. We all know that there were other factors involved with that . . . namely Cyra. In my opinion, if Cyra was not a factor, I believe that Aenon and Avala would have had a successful rulership and lasting marriage. I don't think that's a problem with the Windmasters because the situation is not applicable. We believe in change catapulting growth. However, because the Aenon situation was a tragedy, the rest of the world may have a serious problem with the idea of another Legend marrying a ruler. That's what I believe your parents wanted me to realize . . . although I was already aware of these facts. They have been out of the loop for a while. I will have an accurate feeling after the dinner."

"I never thought about that," Aqila murmured and swallowed hard. "Kavi, if it comes to it—"

"You had better not complete that sentence." He cut her off. "If it comes to it, I won't be the next ruler of Kashmala, and I have no problems with that."

"Kavi - don't - you have worked so hard for this - your parents' expectation. You're their choice for succession.

They want this for you. Think of how horrible I would feel knowing that I robbed you of your destiny for my selfish desires."

Kavi chuckled, "Do you hear yourself? Great love requires great sacrifice. When I first asked my father about marrying you, he said, 'A ruler has never married a seer before. Her training could take years. How will you wait that long? How do you know it's love and not lust? Will you fight for her tomorrow, like you fight for her now?' I told him I would not accept a future for myself where you were not my wife. I was ready to give up being a ruler then and there. We both know that there is a governing class. Several people are qualified for the position and would rule Kashmala well. Succession would never be a problem. Actually, truth be told, my parents wanted me to be the WindGuardian and Saar to succeed them." Kavi laughed.

"However, neither of us liked the idea of that. It took a while, but our parents eventually came around. Aqila, your stars were set in place when you were born to be a seer and a Legend. You can't change that. I don't have to be a ruler to live a great life. I have plenty of talents and strengths. I could be a teacher, scientist, political consultant, or whatever. But I can't live a great and fulfilling life without you. I'm honored that you would sacrifice the cries of your heart, but that will not be necessary. I will make sure of it."

She beamed with love. "I understand Kavi. However, your dream is to rule these lands like your father before you. I know that. You have worked hard all your life for that, and I want that for you. I wish I could do my part at dinner, but trust I will support your decisions faithfully."

"I never question your support. Just know that all other dreams come second to exchanging wedding vows with you." He looked down. "I will meet you at the border in a few minutes." Sterling spiraled down toward the Capitol. Talon and Aqila flew off toward the border shared with Theyra. Hearing Kavi's determination for marriage eased Aqila's mind.

As Talon hovered over the cliff-like terrain of the border, Aqila wondered how Boaz had fared. He must have been successful in retrieving Jai since he was at Tora's house. She silently prayed that nothing else would happen to anyone before she arrived.

CHAPTER 21

Tora's house was completely quiet. Boaz and Tora didn't want to put their worst fears about Jai and Zay into the atmosphere. While the Flamethrowers didn't want to entertain anything worse than what they had already experienced. Everyone was uneasy.

Tora walked inside the room with Boaz and plopped on the floor. "I know I shouldn't be saying this, but this is boring. Sitting around watching two people battle with death with no clear next step."

"I hope Sheraga and Arrow come back soon. That would at least be a start. Sheraga might know what's wrong with Jai and Zay. Arrow will be able to gather his team, I heard them arguing down there."

"Yeah, I did too. My concern is whoever is after Jai; I don't want them to be my problem. I have enough I'm dealing with already."

"Aren't you the leader of this place?"

"Kindle? Yeah, I'm the leader. This is not really what I wanted, but duty called me. Things were running amuck after Father passed. I tried to lead behind the scenes for a while. But that didn't work out. Everyone wanted me to lead and follow in my father's footsteps. Don't get me wrong, I love Kindle and the people. I would just rather be hands-on, working to advance instead of being solely accountable for the well-being of the territory. The Kindlers supported me all the way. Pyroc is our ally. Sheraga has been like the brother I never had. He really helped me get on my feet. However, Ember was not happy. They have opposed us all the way. Then Theyra, no offense to you, has been pressing my border for land, creating tension."

"I know. Theyra is in a crisis. We are still in a civil war. Those who can escape the city are finding refuge on Kindle's border and pressing into your territory. If the civil war would end, then the people could go back to the city. Not making excuses, but they are just fighting for their lives at this point. I live on the opposite side of Theyra, closer to Kashmala. I know I'm a Landkeeper and an enemy to you, but I believe in justice for all people. My best friend is a Windmaster, and I have tried to apply justice to all I meet."

"I understand all of that, I do. Kindle doesn't have a lot of land in general. If we did, I'd have no problem with the Landkeepers having that area. But trying to negotiate with Ember has been nearly impossible. Pyroc has land near my border, but it isn't producing land. Trust me, I'd rather make peace than war. I didn't believe you when you said you were friends with Aqila. But now, I understand. And for the record, you are not an enemy to me."

The pair heard a knock on the door. Tora quickly stood up. "You stay here. I don't want anyone to know you're here." Tora briskly left the room and hurried downstairs.

The Flamethrowers were standing up, looking uneasy. If someone was looking for trouble, the Flamethrowers would be in a bad way. Tora walked between them, "All of you get to one side of the door, right now." There was another knock. He proceeded to the door and slowly opened it, careful to keep the Flamethrowers out of sight.

"It took you long enough. I almost thought something had happened." Sheraga pushed his way inside. "Wow, you all look alive and well."

Tora groaned. "I don't think anyone is in the mood for sarcasm."

Arrow slowly entered after Sheraga. The Flamethrowers gasped and ran to him all at once. Everyone except for Cahya, whose eyes were locked on the thin chain around his neck.

"Arrow, we're so glad you're okay."

"I knew you'd come back!"

"Is Calida coming?"

"Jai is upstairs. We don't know how he's feeling, though."

Arrow felt like he was suffocating in the words and embraces of his team. He wanted to push them away, but he didn't have the strength to do so.

A raspy, commanding voice overtook the others as the door closed, "Everybody, hold up! I know this feels like a reunion, but this is business." Aqila's silver eyes pierced the room. Everyone fell silent. "Tora, you and Sheraga go upstairs. I'll meet you shortly."

Sheraga sighed, "Usually, we're the ones giving the orders, Storm, but given the circumstances, we'll be on our way. I need to check on Jai's condition anyway." Sheraga and Tora steadily proceeded upstairs. Once they were gone, Aqila motioned for Arrow to speak.

Arrow took a deep breath. His eyes were red and swollen, and his face was etched with grief and pain. His hands shook uncontrollably as he spoke. "First, I want to thank all of you for giving your all during the battle. Everyone worked hard to secure the goal and Sitara was freed. However, this battle came with a heavy price. At this time, I must acknowledge that Calida and Beamer lost their lives during the battle." His grief was palpable, and the room was suffused with a heavy, mournful silence as everyone present shared in his sorrow.

The silence was followed by a roaring commotion. The twins began to cry. Yuuna fell to her knees in absolute shock. Suvan, whose demeanor was always vibrant and positive, looked blank.

"So, is Cahya our leader now?" Suvan asked.

"No, he is. Arrow's the leader. Calida gave him the leadership chain. I'm leaving." Cahya stormed past everyone before violently shouldering Arrow, who tried to block the door.

"Cahya, wait!" Arrow called to him. Cahya ignored Arrow. An aura of anger surrounded him as he headed for the streets of Kindle.

Aqila hurried after him. She knew the heavy pain of grief and loss. "Cahya—"

"Leave me alone." A violent flame dusted near her face. Aqila dodged it with ease.

"I only want to offer you a space where you can express all that you are feeling."

Cahya slowly turned to her. His body was tense as he tried to hold back his tears, his every breath shallow and labored. Cahya's hands were clenched into fists, his knuckles white with the effort of holding in his grief. Despite his struggle, he refused to give in to his emotions, determined to stay strong. "She was my sister. I got the hell knocked out of me only to wake up and learn that my sister is dead. You don't have a sister, Aqila! You don't have a family! They gave you up for a greater destiny. But I swore to the Stars that I would protect mine. I promised Calida that nothing bad would happen to our family. I promised!"

Despite his efforts to hold back his tears, they streamed down his face as he tried to articulate his feelings. "It didn't have to end like this. She wouldn't listen to me. I told her that it wasn't a good idea to take on Agni! She wouldn't listen! I begged her to come with me to save Mom. I begged, Aqila!" He shook the seer's shoulders as he frantically searched her eyes.

"We even fought it out! Then I left, I was going to free Mom myself and return to the Flamethrowers. But no, Calida had to do things her way! Up to the last minute, I told her not to go after Agni, but she wouldn't listen! I watched my sister die. And I let that bastard who murdered her get away. They didn't have to die. I fought beside Beamer. He was so young; he was fifteen. They didn't have to die."

That was the fork. The entire situation was flipped solely by Calida's decision.

"Cahya, no one knew your sister better than you. I didn't know her personally, but I don't believe she would have ever fought for something that she didn't believe was right. She paid for her choices with her life. Give yourself time to heal. You were the best brother you could have been to her." Peering down at him she whispered, "She died knowing how much you loved her and your family."

"You can't imagine what I sacrificed to help her with the Flamethrowers."

"The Stars know. Her spirit ascended to the stars by the will of the Universe. As long as you don't forget, her memory will live on."

Cahya nodded before gently shouldering past her. Aqila sighed. She placed her hand over her heart, taking a moment to acknowledge how much it ached. She closed her eyes and remembered Zeroun, she held onto the last laugh they shared. Taking a deep breath, she stepped back into Tora's house. The atmosphere was plagued with tears and sorrow.

Aqila hated what she was seeing. She waited several minutes for Arrow to command their attention. However, he was no better than the rest. "Stand up, all of you! Make one single file line, right now!"

The Flamethrowers hurried into a line, everyone standing straight and tall. "I want you to stand there and think. If you had died in battle, what would Calida be doing right now? What would Calida be saying? Would she be doing nothing? Would she be falling apart? Or would she be pressing forward in your name? Think about it. Think about what's at stake here. Jai is upstairs fighting for his life. You're supposed to help and protect him like this? What are you?"

"I'm a Fireheart, through and through," Suvan replied immediately.

"Likewise, I am a Fireheart," Yuuna replied.

"What about Cahya?" Arin asked.

"He needs some time. Calida was your leader, but she was his sister. He deserves the space and time to process his grief and look to the Universe to guide him," Aqila replied. "Agni is not going to stop. And unfortunately, he is not alone in his pursuit. I discovered this when I was kidnapped in Avala recently. Thankfully the Universe never left me, and I am standing cured today. I have to tend to Jai and catch him up. What are your next steps?"

"I buried Calida and Beamer in the forest. Dysis and Quiver have already started relocating our headquarters to a different part of the forest. Agni may have his cronies attack there. I think we need to go home and gather ourselves to plan our next steps as a team. If Cahya chooses to rejoin us, we will be easy for him to find," Arrow instructed.

"Is it wise to leave Jai here?" Arin asked.

"He will be safe with us, Arin," Aqila replied. She found her question odd. Certainly Jai would be safe with Sheraga, Tora, and herself. Only a mindless fool would dare attack the residence of the leader of Kindle.

Everyone started to move out except for Alena. Aqila approached her before heading to the stairs. "You're not going with them?"

"No, Zay is upstairs too. He was on Agni's side at first, but when he found out that Agni lied about the purpose of their mission, he tried to help us. He saved me twice. It would be wrong to not see if he makes it or not. So, I'm staying here."

CHAPTER 22

"I see. If you're staying, I hope you will fill me in on the lies that Agni told that made Zay change sides," Aqila inquired.

"Of course," Alena whispered before sitting on the couch. Aqila continued upstairs, where she was met by Tora.

"Your friend is in there." He pointed. Just as Aqila approached the room, Boaz bolted out.

"You're safe. I was worried about you! I'm sorry I didn't look for you sooner." Boaz pulled her into a bear hug. As they pulled apart, they looked at each other with a mixture of relief and happiness, thrilled to be in each other's company again.

"Boaz, this wasn't your fault. You did a great service to the world. You did everything right! Kavi told me everything you were going through, and I couldn't be more blessed than to have you as my friend." Aqila looked toward Tora and followed them, slowly leaving Boaz with Zay.

Aqila's heart nearly broke upon seeing Jai lying motionless. She was positive that this was an effect of poisoning.

"I've done everything I could do. I haven't seen anything like this. The shoulder wound is nearly healed. His heart is racing, which is a concern. If it keeps up like this, his heart could just stop."

"I have lightning. If his heart stops I can give him a jolt," Tora offered.

"That won't be necessary," Aqila spoke.

"Can you help him?" Tora asked.

"Yes, I have the antidote for this," She reached into her pants pocket and pulled out a vial with a golden liquid. She opened Jai's mouth slightly and placed five drops on his tongue. "I'm positive this will work. His tongue was blue. Just like mine."

"Like yours? Antidote?" Sheraga questioned.

Instantaneously, Jai started twitching. He took a long breath. His chest could be seen moving in sync with his breathing for the first time. Aqila leaned over him and gave him another five drops.

"How will you know when he's had enough," Tora asked.

"When he's able to open his eyes. What you witnessed is the effect of poisoning by a tranquilizer. It was made for large sea life like whales and sharks. If used on humans, it causes paralysis followed by death."

Jai began to stir after receiving a second dose of the antidote. His eyes began to flutter.

"This is a serious problem if Agni has access to something like this. This would allow him to level the playing field in battle—in domains where he doesn't have the manpower to win. With this in his back pocket, he's a serious threat now . . . even to Pyroc," Sheraga reflected.

"I agree," Tora sighed, "like I really need another problem right now. Especially one coming from Ember."

"Well, I've been suggesting that you take Agni seriously from the start." Aqila rolled her eyes.

"Yeah, and if you had told me this, I would have had a more listening ear."

"Well, I'm a seer, bottom line, so you should have taken it seriously the whole time," Aqila insisted.

"You know I would have loved to take this seriously!" Sarcasm oozed from Tora's voice. "How come this is my first time hearing about this from either of you?"

"Because it didn't involve you, I didn't see you in the vision. I only saw Agni's plans for Sheraga. Tora, you know me. I would have made the trip if I thought something was coming."

Jai groaned as he struggled to get up.

Aqila was quickly by his side. "Take it easy now. How do you feel?"

Jai gulped several times before responding, "Stiff as fiery hell."

"What happened?" Tora asked.

"What do you mean? Obviously, they got served-"

"Are you done?" Aqila cut Sheraga off.

The DragonLord shrugged his shoulders.

"I remember. I remember what happened to me—the reason I can't remember my family or where I'm from. But how did I get here? What happened?"

"You were injected with a tranquilizer, and it left you paralyzed. You would have been dead by morning. I had been injected with it too. That's how I had some of the antidote left," Aqila explained.

"Okay, one, can I please be filled in? Think of it as my repayment for you and your friends exhausting my medical supplies," Tora insisted.

"That means . . . we lost. We tried to fight Agni and lost. He had a following ready to fight to the death on his behalf. The Flamethrowers! Is everyone else okay?"

"Everyone is coming along to the best of their ability. Now, I need to leave and update my guard as to what is going on. Jai, rest up. You'll need it. Tora, Aqila, I'll be taking my leave." Sheraga turned on his heels and left the room.

"Tora, could you make Jai something to eat, quickly? It will aid the antidote."

"Yeah, I'll be back. Jai, you like eggs?"

"You know it! We Firehearts love our eggs."

Tora left the pair alone.

A few minutes passed. "What's up? You wanted us alone for a reason." Jai groaned as he stretched his neck.

"I did. I have something important to tell you that has to be kept between us. I'm a Legend Seer."

"A what? Is that possible? No, don't answer that, obviously it is. So what does that mean?"

"I'm a Seer and a Legend. I was kidnapped and taken to Avala. I had to fight my way to freedom, and that's when I felt an incredible surge of power and strength. Then I went through the process to complete my apprenticeship, and that's when it was revealed to me. I am the Windmaster Legend."

"Well, that makes two of us, and it's great that we already know each other. We're halfway there. That's positive, and it also poses a problem. Agni's big agenda is to kill all of the Legends."

"I figured as much. Well, I'm planning to keep my identity as a Legend under wraps. I've only told you outside of my immediate family and my fiancé's family. I need to tell a close friend of mine so he knows what he's getting himself into. However, I believe that being a seer is enough for now. But, there's bad news, Agni isn't acting alone."

There was a knock on the door. Jai looked to Aqila before replying, "Come in."

Boaz opened the door and slowly entered, "I heard that you were doing better and wanted to speak. I'm Boaz of

Theyra, and it's good to see you awake now. Everyone was looking rough at the border." Boaz leaned against the wall on the far side of the room.

Jai sat up and extended his hand. "Nice to meet you." Boaz walked over and accepted the handshake. "You must have picked us up at the border. Thanks, you helped save my life."

"Anytime, I just like to be useful."

"Jai, this is my best friend, Boaz. Bo, stay. I want to catch you up too."

Boaz leaned on the door near Aqila. "What is it?"

"I'm a full seer now. Zeroun passed this afternoon."

Boaz gasped at the revelation, "I can't believe it. I'm so sorry, Aqila. I can't imagine how you feel." He touched her shoulder. "I know how close you two were; I mean, he was like a parent in a lot of ways." He embraced his tall friend.

Aqila's eyes watered. "Thanks, Bo. As Zeroun passed away, he revealed that I am also the Windmaster Legend. He knew the entire time and even said that I needed to go through that ordeal in Avala for me to recognize and accept my destiny. This Waterbearer girl injected me with a whale tranquilizer."

"Whale tranquilizer? Couldn't that have killed you?" Boaz shouted.

"I know. She gave me an entire syringe full, and the only reason I'm alive—"

"Because you're a Legend," Jai finished her sentence. "That's probably why I was able to last. Being a Legend gave us the physical strength to resist the full effects of the poisoning. But if Agni is not alone, who is helping him?"

"Agni is not alone. What!" Boaz was shocked.

Aqila shook her head. "No, he's not acting alone. He has a partner, and his name is Neptune."

TO TAIL A SEER

The reddish-brown feathers of a red-tailed hawk blew in the brisk wind. The feathers were exquisitely detailed, with a range of colors from ivory and red to deep brown and black, all blending together in a harmonious symphony. The wind ruffled the feathers, causing them to shift and twirl as if in a state of constant motion.

Inhale. Exhale. Its rider sat calmly on its back, taking in the scent in the air with his eyes closed. His long legs were covered in soot gray harem pants. His silver-colored tunic was of average length and closely resembled the Wind Guardian's style, except for the metal mesh overshirt. The man's fawn-colored skin had copper undertones. Long, wavy dark gray hair was pulled back into an immaculate single braid. The winds eased, and to this, his piercing deep gray eyes opened. Their dark stormy hue almost bordered on black.

After adjusting the pair of daggers secured in his belt, he reached for the reins of his dasher. The hawk's feathers fanned out behind it like the tail of a comet shooting across the sky. He beckoned the hawk to fly higher, flashing symmetrical red tattoos on his hands. The tattoos were of feathers. They were a deep, dark shade of crimson, each one perfectly placed and carefully inked. The patterns flowed across the man's skin like a dance, the feathers appearing to take flight with every movement of his hands. Despite the boldness of the red ink, they had a delicate quality to them, each one crafted with great attention to detail. It was a striking contrast to the man's rough hands.

Rising over the rocky terrain of Theyra, he inhaled deeply. Following the exhale, he found the scent he was after and vowed to never lose it. "According to the rest of the world, the Windmasters don't have problems. However, our clan never gets equality. Maybe she will fix it. She storms; she must at least have a touch of our blood. But if she won't fix it I will, won't I, Vermilion?" The red-tailed hawk squawked in response to its master. "Yes, my loyal girl. We will restore our clan to its former glory. Whatever it takes."

He soared high into the sky over Theyrian lands, never losing track of the scent. He picked up her scent from the mountains and imprinted it into his mind. He now knew her by smell alone.

His lips parted. His mouth watered ever so slightly, "Vermilion, it seems like we will touch down in Kindle. Oh, Aqila, destiny has been kind to you. A seer and a Legend, quite the catch. I. Will. Find. You."

S he covered her face with a black hooded cape as she carefully tipped through the busy mountain city of Kashmala, an anomaly among dazzling silver hues. The sky was the most ethereal shade of blue and the off white clouds felt close enough to graze with her fingertips. She could not afford to revel in the striking beauty of the landscape for too long. There was too much to do and much too little time.

She had never experienced anything like this. The world she knew was wrath and fury, yet this atmosphere was peaceful. The chatter, the laughter, everything seemed to blend in the most perfect symphonic harmony. She was drowning in a sea of silverish hair, stormy gray eyes, and the constant squawking of massive birds perfectly suited for riding.

The glowing shimmer of her golden eyes focused on the majestic Capitol. She was overwhelmed by the gray marble building. It was an old relic of a distant past, with its carvings and spires. The gray marble steps to the entrance seemed to beckon her forward, yet her feet refused to move. Shaking her head briskly, she took a reluctant step forward, knowing quite well that she must make haste.

"Cyra?" A deep voice called her name.

She slowly turned around, "Basir," she whispered as her eyes watered. Several years of memories flooded her consciousness. The good and the ugly. Fighting back tears, she let her hood fall back, revealing her face. Her jet black hair fell just past her shoulders.

He hasn't changed.

She took in his bronze skin and sharp gray eyes that resembled the color of steel. His broad shoulders filled his long sky blue tunic with closures matching his white harem pants. Long locks of straight dark gray hair were neatly pulled into a low ponytail, falling well past his waist.

Instead of anger for everything that had transpired between them, the gaze Basir held was one of calm and comfort. When he smirked, the tears that she fought so desperately to withhold could no longer be contained.

Cyra ran and embraced Basir. The warmth of his body eased her heavy heart. His deep chuckle warmed her soul as he held her close.

"It's okay, Cyra. It's okay."

As if he read my mind.

Pulling away from him, Cyra dried her eyes.

"How did you know it was me?"

"Come on! You're the shortest thing around here."

She playfully punched his arm.

Basir smiled rubbing his arm, "Well, it was actually this hideous article of clothing, hood, shawl, cape, whatever this nonsense is."

"Basir! It makes me look distinguished."

"It actually doesn't, but..."

Cyra laughed. It felt good to laugh. She actually couldn't remember the last time she had a hearty laugh.

"I know you wanted to see me, shall we consult inside the Capitol?"

"I'd rather not," Cyra looked down at her hands.

"Okay well, let's take a walk."

"Sure."

"On one condition, it's imperative that you remove that eye sore."

"Just as obnoxious as the day I met you," Cyra scoffed. She removed her hood and gently draped it across her arm.

"Call me whatever, let's stroll."

Cyra hurried to his side as the pair took a walk toward the lush rolling hills of Wyndhm. It felt odd to walk beside him. She was swallowed by his massive shadow.

"So what's going on? I'd heard much, but I'd rather have the facts straight from the source."

Straight to the point as always.

"How have you been, Basir? I'm always talking about me and my problems, my ideas, my visions. I never ask about you."

"How gracious of you." A long silence came between them. Basir sighed, "I am doing okay, average at best."

I know how you feel.

"I heard you got married."

Basir smiled wide, "I did. Honestly, I didn't deserve her."

"I know she doesn't feel that way."

"Yeah, I know. Nephele and I have loved each other since we were teenagers. She's the owner of my heart. I just knew that I ruined that after I caused Ila's death. I know it was an accident, but she was my best friend. It weighs on my heart to know that she never got to experience the happiness that I'm experiencing... and it's my fault."

"She did get to experience happiness, Basir. She felt love and friendship and happiness because of you. You meant the world to her."

He swallowed hard, I know. I didn't realize how she felt until it was a whirlwind. I was so blinded by it and confused. I tried to dissuade her. My heart was already taken and I only saw her as a friend -"

"You don't have to explain any of that to me. You know that I know." Once again there was silence.

"I'm here because I need help. My daughter is on a troubled path."

"I'm sorry to hear that, have you consulted with Zeroun?"

"I have. He did not see a solution in our lifetime. Me and Aenon marrying and having the twins has initiated a -"

"A blood curse. Damn. I tried to intervene before something like this happened," Basir hung his head.

"I know, you did try. But I was already pregnant when you and Ila crashed the meeting at the Beach tribe."

"I figured as much."

"What?"

"Yes, that was the reason I walked away from the challenge that Aenon initiated. I would never fight a pregnant woman and put innocent unborn children at risk. That's why I walked away. Ila was furious about it, but I had no intention of sharing something with anyone that I had not confirmed. I chose not to ask in case the Beach tribe didn't know that you two were in a relationship."

"I'm sorry, Basir."

"That's the past, Cyra. What can be done for your daughter? What do you need from me?"

"Zeroun said a chaotic power will awaken in Soleil. She and her descendants will suffer. The second born of her bloodline will be gifted with exceptional abilities that they will struggle to control. Solar eclipses will awaken the curse in full force. Death by lightning will be unavoidable until the curse is broken. I don't know what I should do."

Basir grimaced, "Blood curses are always bad. And they have unforeseen consequences on other people."

"The only thing I can do is to try and help Soleil... or end her. That came from Zeroun."

"Can't argue with a Seer. There are no lies in their sight. I'm curious as to how she will have chaotic power. I thought your children were giftless."

"They were... after we learned that Selene was dead. Soleil went through a horrible emotional breakdown. She commanded fire for the first time, but she never did it again. After she learned that I caused her father's death and we were forced to flee, her eyes... changed color. She has light brown eyes now. And when she's angry she can command fire, but it's wild and unruly. Any semi-experience person could easily subdue her."

"This is something else. This could completely change the way we should perceive the giftless. Maybe all giftless people have weakened, dormant abilities and there is a trigger that unleashes it. I need some time, we both have work to do. Zeroun mentioned a solar eclipse for a reason, it's important. I will check with the astronomers to see if we can pinpoint the next solar eclipse. We need to research our respective people's histories to see if we have any other cases of something like this."

"Other cases?"

"Yes, sadly, people have intermixed abilities before... it never ends well. Maybe the Firehearts or Waterbearers have an account of this. If all else fails we go to the sages. Please, Cyra, keep your faith this time. We will do everything we can to save her, if there ends up being no other option... only you can end her. Hold your faith. Promise me that."

The pair stopped at the top of the beautiful hills of Wyndhm. It was like paradise. All could be seen was grass and sky along with the occasional animal frolicked about.

Cyra sighed and forced back a sob. She covered her mouth with her hands. Glancing at Basir from the corner of her eye, he just stood relaxed with his hands gently clasped behind his back. Years ago, he would have demanded an answer. He would have pushed his point and his proof, mentally exhausted her until she bent a knee admitting he was right. But this patience of his was new to her.

He has grown so much.

She dried her eyes. *So have I.*

"I promise."